The Case
⁓of the⁓
Carnaby
Castle
Curse

THE FOURTH ANTY BOISJOLY MYSTERY

The Case of the Carnaby Castle Curse

1. Telephone, Telegram, Tell a Boisjoly 1
2. Nothing Worse Than a Curse Behind in its Work 9
3. Riches Which Pitch Witches into Deep Ditches.........19
4. A Peek at the Peaks of Peak From a Peaky Peak 29
5. The Brisk Business of Being Boisjoly....................39
6. The Many and Mounting Motives for Murder..........48
7. The Unstoppable Start for the Top of the Scarp........58
8. The Legion Layers of Lint...................................68
9. It All Began at Christmas in Milan 77
10. The Darkly Arbitrary Devil's Emissary 85
11. What Lies in Wait Beyond the Graveyard Gate 94
12. Purgatory's Category of Vainglory Allegory 103
13. Loftis' Lonely Lot in Life 116
14. No Man is Immune to the Italian Moon................123
15. Setting the Betting on an Early June Wedding 133
16. The Deceptive Exterior of the Future Anterior..........141
17. Seek No Further a Passage to Murder...................151
18. Bones, Stones, and Crones
    What Moans Alone in the Catacombs 157
19. A Better Belter Belstead 166
20. The Mystery of the Missing Memoir 178
21. Luckily Armed With a Lucky Charm 185
22. The Twist in the Mist......................................189
Anty Boisjoly Mysteries....................................202

CHAPTER ONE

Telephone, Telegram, Tell a Boisjoly

I'VE ONLY EVER KNOWN one club steward who's killed a man.

It could be fairly assumed that by then, what with my breadth of experience of the form, they'd number in the dozens, and yet here we are.

The Juniper Gentleman's Club is the most gentlemanly and the most clubby in the city and the reason for that was always Carnaby, London's finest club steward. Under his captaincy things always ticked along in mild, mannered, Mayfair moderation and, consequently, during his annual vacation (earlier this 1929, should posterity find itself wondering) there had been a notable turn of Piccadilly pandemonium. The afternoon when it all began — and this is just an example, mind — Bumper Wise-Millsip made it all the way to the tea room with no one reminding him that he was still wearing his bowler.

I was pondering Bumper's bowler — and what looked to be an elm leaf trapped in his spat — when Carnaby's thankfully short-term stand-in clomped up to my starboard side like a child wearing adult shoes. He arranged the scotch and seltzer and then, amazingly but expectedly, did violence on my whisky with a prolonged spritz of soda. I sighed in fond memory of Carnaby's perfect pour and took up the glass.

"Thank you, Hallowit," I said magnanimously and viewed the maroon and mahogany salon of the Juniper through the parallax of my almost entirely clear glass of mainly undiluted soda water.

Every club steward has his signature style, of course, and I don't judge, it just happens that where Carnaby would deliver the mixture soundlessly and softly and then fade away, as ash on the wind, Hallowit's practice was to linger at my elbow, like the haunting presence of a bull buffalo that I'd wronged in some previous life.

Finally he gathered the courage to clear his throat.

"Was there something else, Hallowit?" I asked.

"In fact, there was something, if I may, Mister Bossjolly." Hallowit spoke as the man he was — one of those sedulous graduates of the East End who never condescend to obscure their proud fish-monger heritage with the diaphanous veil of diction. By 'Bossjolly', I expect, he meant the family affliction, 'Boisjoly'. Anthony Quilfeather Boisjoly, to map it all out in a mouthful — Anty, to my friends, and 'Bossjolly' among the murmuring community of dockworkers from which the Juniper recruits its temporary stewards.

"Actually it's pronounced 'Beaujolais', like the wine region," I said, helpfully. "Only one of many fiercely counter-intuitive surnames gifted us by our shared Norman heritage."

"Yes, Mister Bossjolly. Of course."

"Boisjoly."

"Bore-july."

"Nearer," I encouraged. "No, actually, that's worse. It's Boisjoly."

"Bwahjolly."

"Boisjoly. In fact, can we go back to Bossjolly? It seems a solid working compromise. Like one of those Rembrandts by Van Gogh — distant enough the original to not be taken for a poor forgery."

Hallowit looked vaguely uncomfortable. He clearly had some important problem preying upon his mind and he needed to share it with an adult more concerned with the smooth operation of the Juniper and less with the pronunciation of a decidedly tricky surname. He had selected me, no doubt, from among the snoozing snowy belfries of the Juniper salon because, unlike them, I am young and slim and chestnut of hair and clear of complexion, and I was awake.

"It's Mister Carnaby, sir," he said at last.

"Yes?"

"He has yet to return from his holiday."

"Yes," I acknowledged, trying and failing to keep the low melancholy from my voice. "I know."

There was something in Hallowit's manner that gave me to suspect that there was more on his docket than Carnaby's holiday arrangements, and indeed what he was about to impart was to come to be far, far graver than either of us understood in the moment.

"He was meant to have returned yesterday, sir," he said. "And... you see, there's a telegram."

"Well, there you have it, Hallowit. The key to deciphering the meaning hidden in a telegram, in my long experience of receiving them, is to read it. What does Mister Carnaby say in his telegram?"

Hallowit glanced furtively about the salon and lowered his voice. "The message isn't from Mister Carnaby, sir — it's for him."

"Ah, I see your dilemma now," I said. "Does it appear to be urgent?"

Hallowit's doughy countenance took on a pained expression, like an otherwise innocent brioche with a guilty secret. "I feel I need to explain, sir, that I was looking for the address of our syphon merchant — there's been an unanticipated increase in consumption, of late — and I found this." He lowered his tray that I might see that lain upon it was a telegram.

"I admire your professional ethics enormously, Hallowit," I assured him, "but you needn't worry yourself. Telegrams are widely recognised as public communiqués — it's why I'm always at pains to craft mine and include at least one original witticism. I like to know that I'm expanding the horizons of the cable clerks and page boys of the metropolis."

To illustrate the point, I took up the paper and read the following disturbing missive:

"THE CURSE IS ONCE AGAIN UPON THE CARNABY FAMILY-(STOP)-DO NOT RETURN TO HOY-(STOP)-ONLY DEATH AWAITS YOU"

This was curious enough. More curious still was the postmark, 'W. Carnaby, member, Juniper Club, Mayfair, London.' It was unsigned and it was dated several days prior to Carnaby's departure.

"Do you happen to know where Mister Carnaby has gone for his vacation, Hallowit?"

"He has returned home, sir, to the town of Hoy."

ੴ

"Pack our monocle polish and other essentials, Vickers," I said to my man only a vertiginous taxi flight later at the Boisjoly bijoux residence in Kensington. "Tonight we hoy for Hoy."

"Very good sir," said Vickers from behind a collapsible ironing board in the kitchen, on which he appeared to be working the creases out of an opera glove. I didn't enquire why nor, more bafflingly, where he found a single opera glove, because I knew that by then he would have long forgotten. Vickers is a gentleman's gentleman among gentlemen's gentlemen and has been for at least three generations of Boisjoly patriarchs, and while everything that passed his field of vision up to and including the coronation of George IV remains limpid and limber recollection, his intimacy with current events had since become a lively field of delightful surprises. Otherwise, the man is as correct as the pluperfect and presents like a tall, proud birch tree, dressed for the theatre.

4

"Would that be the seaside town of Hoi in Wirral, sir, or the village of Hoy in the Peak District?" asked Vickers, somewhat distractedly as he picked up the opera glove and looked at it as though wondering where it came from.

"You know, it didn't occur to me to ask," I said. "It's the spawning ground of Carnaby, Juniper club steward. Does that help?"

"I fear not."

"Does this?" I produced and passed Vickers the telegram.

"This is Hoy, spelt with a Y, in the Peak District." Vickers scrutinised the paper with a brow furrowed with offended feudal sensibilities. "W. Carnaby, member..."

"Yes, I noticed that. Whoever sent that cable had cause to believe that Carnaby is a member of the Juniper. It's only part of the intrigue which draws us north."

"I shall pack immediately."

"And I shall dress leisurely."

❦

My favourite London train station is invariably whichever I'm in when the question comes up. That afternoon, consequently, as we boarded our train on her famous platform eight (under which, it is reported, Queen Boudica is buried) there was no greater supporter than I of the candidacy of Kings Cross in the tight race for London's jolliest terminal. It's out of these grand ornate arches are we launched to points north on the Flying Scotsman to Edinburgh and the Peterborough exchange to the unspoilt reaches of Skegness. It's mainly the crowds that captivate, though, the calculated chaos of a busy train station — and there are none busier than Kings Cross — of ten thousand individual paths crossing, each with its own, unique destination, dancing and dashing to a platform, a train, car, a compartment, a place therein, then off at the speed of steam to another station, there met by a loved one and whisked to an exact address and a

5

specific seat behind a precise pork pie, and all this mind-boggling logistical magic is performed beneath the Victorian knack for transforming brick and iron into the baroque. Yes, I'm going to go with Kings Cross.

Day passed into evening in that twinkly way it has and the sooty, smoky air of urban London soon gave way to the sooty, dusty air of suburban Luton. The yellow windows of happy homes zipped by our window, the train chugged rhythmically and Vickers snoozed in time with it. Our compartment was starboard — normally an excellent vantage point from which to view blurry scenery — but as the sun was setting magnificently and habitually in the west, I glanced toward it just as a shadowy figure briefly blocked the orange spectacle and passed out of sight down the corridor. Something about the chap — his trenchcoat or low-brimmed fedora or furtive movements — aroused the Boisjoly instinct for intrigue and incident, and I pursued.

I poked my head into the corridor in time to see the figure disappear, in a dashing flash of gabardine and raucous roar of engine and wind, through the doors to the next car.

I followed. There's nothing like passing between two clattering train cars in brisk, blowing twilight to make one feel like Douglas Fairbanks, though not quite so jowly, obviously. I recommend the activity very highly.

He had vanished. This led me to conclude that either he was some sort of phantom or that his compartment was in this car. I moved casually along the corridor, taking a surreptitious census as I passed through the carriage. First compartment was a round robust family and their nurse laying out an elaborate picnic on a valise. I made note to check on their progress at some later point. Next compartment — empty, adding keen support to the phantom theory.

The third compartment foiled my investigations entirely — the curtains were drawn. I closed an eye and endeavoured to take in what I could through a gap in the drapery and, as I focused, the lights went out. We had entered a tunnel and all was darkness and the explosive echo of steel wheels and hurtling locomotive.

6

The whistle screeched, as they will in tunnels, as a prelude for returning to the open air, and in that same instant the lights came back on and I was face-to-face with my phantom.

"Hello, Inspector." I smiled broadly and sincerely at Inspector Ivor Wittersham of Scotland Yard, with whom I have shared many adventures and, even if it's me saying so, developed a warm working relationship of mutual admiration.

"What the devil are you doing on this train, Boisjoly?" asked Ivor as he slid open the door of his compartment.

"Sixty miles an hour, give or take," I speculated. Of course, like Ivor, I was pleased to no end at this chance encounter, but plagued nevertheless by the suspicion that chance had little to do with it. Indeed, the very first time I met Ivor was on board a train bound for Fray, scene of the twin mysteries which so vexed the Canterfell family last year. This was the beginning of the machine-like collaboration of Ivor's professional interest and my meddling curiosity. I didn't recognise him as a police officer, then, and assumed, what with his no-man's-land trench coat, slap-dash moustache, and low-brow lidding, that he sold foundation garments door-to-door and lived with his mother.

"I'm on an important recovery mission to the town of Hoy, in the Peak District," I confided.

Ivor stood away from the door and beckoned me to take a seat in his otherwise empty compartment.

"And just what is it that you're recovering in Hoy?" he asked, taking the place across from me.

"Stewards," I said. "There's a positive run on the market in London, at the moment, and I have it on good authority that they grow some of the finest in the market towns of Derbyshire."

Ivor watched me silently, betraying no notion nor expectation, with the expressionless countenance of one who has inured himself to waiting for me to get to the point.

"Our man Carnaby has failed to return from his holiday," I explained.

"And you regard that as suspicious enough to warrant a rescue campaign."

"On its own and in isolation," I said, "I do. Carnaby is the paramount of duty in a dutiful profession. He once loaned Sir Ludlow Royce-Phipps the very trousers off his backside when the poor chap set his own on fire quite accidentally while fencing with a skewer of *brochettes de crevettes flambées,* just before he was meant to give a welcome speech to the Duke of Kent."

"A trouserless steward doesn't sound very correct."

"No one batted an eye," I explained, "when Carnaby appeared in a kilt he'd fashioned for himself out of a clutch of tartan antimacassars. Clan Buchanon, if memory serves. His Highness took it to be some sort of tribute to Balmoral."

Ivor regarded me beneath hooded eyes, as one doubting a tall tale or drifting off to sleep.

"You want to tell me the rest of it?"

"Well, there is this," I conceded, withdrawing the telegram from my breast pocket and handing it over.

"There's a curse?" said Ivor as he examined the paper.

"First I'm hearing of it, but stewards are a notoriously austere breed, particularly with regards living arrangements, family curses, and cocktail recipes."

"This is it?" Ivor held up the telegram. "This is why you're going to Hoy?"

"For the impetuous Boisjoly," I said, "it's enough."

"Then you really don't know."

"Might do," I said circumspectly. "Is it bigger than a breadbox?"

"It's why I, too, am going to Hoy, Mister Boisjoly." Ivor paused while the train clattered over a dramatic set of points. "There's been a murder."

CHAPTER TWO

Nothing Worse Than a Curse Behind in its Work

Ivor was unwilling and, in the main, unable to tell me much more than the welcome revelation that it wasn't Carnaby who had been saved the bother of retirement planning. All he could and would tell me was that the victim of the murder in Hoy had been a woman.

When we arrived in Chesterfield, however, and were collected at the station by a convivial country constable by the name of Blewit, the market in brass tacks began a brisk trade.

"We don't get so many people murdered, up here in the Gateway to the Pennines," said Blewit, an economy-sized constable who spoke his every word as though it were the punchline to a joke he'd been waiting weeks to tell. "Can't really spare them, like you can down in London."

Blewit packed our bags and ourselves haphazardly into a rickety, yellow and black Austin Seven that he called, with disarming familiarity, Gordy, and we drove off into the moonless night.

"Most of the time when there *is* a killing, of course, it's clear who done it," said Blewit, continuing the theme. "Not much call for a detective-inspector from Scotland Yard when the chief suspect is the only one around for a hundred miles in any direction."

Gordy, it's worth noting here, had only the one working headlight and had been adapted to the rocky backroads of the Peak District by long-ago replacing the suspension springs in favour of, it appeared, solid iron blocks. The exchange of ideas was largely confined, therefore, to pithy observations from Blewit and involuntary expressions of distress from me. Vickers suffered in stoic silence and Ivor appeared to be enjoying the ride.

"Have you a suspect in Hoy, Constable?" asked Ivor.

"Not unless you count the curse," said Blewit. "And there's many that do."

"What's all this about a curse?"

"Just your customary ancestral curse, Inspector. Most of these villages have their own folk tales, usually running to witchcraft, family curses, of course, and ghosts. Village up by Bamford Edge has its very own dragon. Lives in the Granny Smith orchard, so they say."

"But no worldly suspects to speak of, then," concluded Ivor.

"That's just it, Inspector, apart from the curse and, I suppose, a conspiracy of practically the entire town, no one *could* have done it. The whole thing was witnessed by six people and they all swear there was no one even near the victim when it happened."

"When what happened, exactly?"

"The victim — the wife of the family patriarch of the castle, you see — was carried off by the mists, to hear witnesses tell it."

"Carried off by the mists? What mists?"

"Well, *the* mists, Inspector." Blewit gestured around us at a gossamer fog floating in layers above the moor. "One moment, she's atop Hoy Scarp, next she's at the bottom. The scarp is a cliff on the opposite side of Hoy Tor, and it's a sheer drop of some hundred feet to a rocky end."

"It's suicide, then," concluded Ivor.

"Recently married, best of spirits according to all accounts, left a half-finished note in her room, telling her mother in what sounded adoring detail about life at the castle…"

"Yes, I see. Most suspicious." Ivor nodded at the passing night. "Recently married to whom?"

"Cecil Carnaby, sir," replied Blewit jovially. "Heir to the family fortune and master of Carnaby Castle."

There's something inherently anticipatory about fresh, night air and near total darkness obscuring unfamiliar rural roads observed from the recesses of a rickety, bouncing Morris Seven. I expect the effect is similar in the Austin Seven or even the Morris Eight, in the right conditions, and it amounts to a child-like, Christmas Eve thrill at the unknown which lays ahead. How will these black hills against the inky sky appear in the light of dawn? What intrigues await us in the cursed town of Hoy? How is it that Carnaby the club steward's ancestral home is, apparently, a castle? Will I be able to sit comfortably again without the aid of a lengthy convalescence?

Finally the twists and lifts and sudden shifts slowed to a long curve before one of the dark hills which slowly contrasted into the form of a little stone village, rendered timeless in the moonlight. Rough stone houses and public buildings arranged themselves along a curving, ascending road as though having tumbled into place at some point in the distant past and, finding themselves comfortable and among convivial company, they set about embedding themselves into the hillside. Most of this presented itself in silhouette, like a shadow theatre, capped at the top of the hill by a monstrous castle composed of menacing towers, cracked and sharpened over the centuries, clawing at the night sky.

Gordy struggled up the stony, deserted main street, losing its grip here and there on the dew-slicked cobblestones, and finally sputtered to a midnight silence before a gritstone pub with small, uneven windows glowing yellow against the night.

"I've made arrangements for you to stay at the castle," said Blewit to Ivor. "I didn't know that you would be bringing friends."

"Mister Boisjoly will no doubt make his own arrangements."

"I'm sure that space can be found for us at the castle." We all gazed at the thing leaning over us. "I have a man on the inside."

"Oh, not the castle," corrected Blewit. Rather, he sounded as though he thought he was setting the record straight, but then went on to say, "I meant the Castle."

"There's another one of those?" I marvelled. "Can't be very big, by comparison."

"That's the Castle right there." Blewit nodded — his arms otherwise occupied with baggage — at the pub. "The Castle Pub and Guest House. Very comfortable, I'm told."

Whoever told Blewit that the Castle Pub and Guest House was very comfortable was, charitably speaking, a shameless liar. The rooms were in an attic retrofitted onto a root cellar sometime in the reign of Edward the Confessor with the chief purpose, apparently, of keeping things cold. The only source of heat was a pint of agreeable bitter consumed below stairs, and the only point in *my* room, at least, where one could stand up straight was beneath a sizable hole in the roof. The bed was comfortable, in a pioneering, outdoorsy sort of way.

Having got that out of my system, the drinks and decor and din of village goodwill gathered in the local managed to offset and then some the discomforts of attic living. Ivor's plan had been to begin his investigation in earnest in the cold light of morning and Vickers had fallen asleep several times during the journey, somehow, and barely made it to his sack of straw before resuming his slumbers. I, however, needed more internal heating fuel and the company of Hoy's chattering class, and so lingered in the bar.

The Castle Pub expressed its cosy and convivial comfort in layers of upholstery and rugs stacked over worn wood and smooth stone in an indiscriminate, organic motif, like an embroidered English garden. The ceiling was low and beamed and the room was warm and ringing with the cheer and chatter of village neighbours who know each other's secrets.

"Pint of your proudest, please, landlord." I leaned on the low bar. Everyone else in the place had, evidently, brought a friend, and so I defaulted to my tried and tested strategy of making the acquaintance of the only person in the place who can't make an excuse.

"Up from London, are you?" asked the landlord as he pulled the pint. "You with that inspector fellow?"

"Only in the sense that we see eye-to-eye on most things," I said. "But he is here in his capacity as official plodder in charge of the investigation, while I come in search of friends, old and new."

"Nasty business, that." The barman was a tall, bony, sturdy sort, grey of hair and complexion, as though by colour and construction intended to be a chimney sweep, switched at birth with the son of an honest innkeeper, he now stoops to serve my pint.

"The murder, you mean," I said, I thought, rhetorically.

"Murder? What murder?"

"Ah, I thought you knew," I said. "Boisjoly, by the way, Anty to my friends and those who hand me pints, who are also my friends, by definition." I offered my hand and the barman took it.

"Odd," he said.

"Not so much as it sounds. It's of Norman origin, I mean, and translates, roughly, as 'Goodwood'."

"Eh?"

"Boisjoly. Not as odd as it sounds, but let us settle on Anty. And you are?"

"Odd, I've just told you."

"Your actual name is Odd?"

"Short for Oddly."

"And why not?" I said. "I'm hardly in a position to pass judgement. Tell me, Odd, if you were unaware that a murder had been committed, to what nasty business did you refer?"

"The curse." Odd placed his hands on the bar and ducked beneath the glassware hanging between us so that he could steady both his eyes on mine. "There's a curse on Carnaby Castle, Anty, and yesterday it claimed the young bride of Cecil Carnaby."

"Lecherous sort of curse, is it? Swept her off her feet?"

"It did just that," Odd assured me. "The mists carried her right over Hoy Scarp, just like the curse used to do in the old days, with much more regularity."

"Oh? That's curious. What caused the curse to fall behind in its work?"

Something in this appeared to strike Odd as disquieting. He swivelled a glance over his shoulder, as though suddenly and inexplicably aware of a ghostly presence or, possibly, a hornet.

"No idea. Couldn't say." Odd retreated, cleared two tankards from the counter, and gave them a cursory rinse in a tin basin. A distinct chill had descended on our hitherto warm rapport and, in an effort to rekindle the flames of friendship, I changed the subject.

"A lot of these Carnabys about then, are there?"

"Only about half the town." Odd tentatively returned to my end of the bar. "I'm a Carnaby."

"Oh, right," I said, and took a deep draw on my bitter while I gave that due consideration. "I had assumed that, what with it being called Carnaby Castle, that it was occupied by all available Carnabys."

"Castle Carnabys." Odd pronounced this obscure distinction with a certain disdain.

"As opposed to…"

"Townies." Odd spread his not inconsiderable wingspan in a manner suggesting that 'townies' applied to all that he surveyed. "Most of us are Town Carnabys. Only Castle Carnabys live in the castle, apart from those that work there."

"What a peculiar arrangement," I observed. "How do you tell them apart? Team jerseys?"

"Castle Carnabys aren't really Carnabys at all, truth be told. Branch of the family built itself a castle and made serfs of their own kin, hundreds of years back."

This went some distance to clearing up an undefinable cavil that had sprung up in my mind since learning that Carnaby the club steward had his own castle.

"Speak of the devil..." spoke Odd of a miasma of whisky fumes and tobacco that moored alongside me at the bar. Our new companion looked as though he'd just woken up in a ditch and popped in for a quick one but not without first freshening up with a roll in another ditch. He had long, stringy hair, a nose like the bulb of a car horn, and that dreamy expression of the man who's raised enough dosh for the milestone ninth glass.

"Ay up," said the arrival, which Odd interpreted to mean, presumably, the usual, which was a sloppy overpour of house whisky.

"You're among the town Carnabys in service at the castle?" I asked, assuming that he was chiefly employed in scaring away the crows.

"Head butler," slurred the scarecrow.

"Not really."

"And why not?"

"Why not indeed?" I agreed. "Tell me, Mister Carnaby, do you know of another Carnaby engaged in a similar capacity at the castle?"

"Could do," sputtered the butler. "Got a name?"

"I don't, actually, just a first initial — W."

"Wurt."

"I beg your pardon?"

"Wurt," repeated the butler. "Only one W Carnaby on staff at the castle. Wurt."

I breakfasted in the bar room on farm fresh eggs, smoked bacon, buttery fruit loaf and tea served on demand by Odd, who kept the kettle on the boil behind the bar. Ivor never joined me and I gave him every opportunity, even lingering over my third cup until it went cold. Finally Odd informed me that the inspector had left for the castle hours ago.

Hoy in the morning is quite different to Hoy at night. It's a bustling little village of clopping horses and shopping townsfolk and squawking merchants. The air was composed of something completely different to that which they supply us in London — some rigorous recipe of nature and farmland and woodfire smoke. The village climbed the hill, mostly on either side of a cobbled, winding road, and the hill itself was on a rise that gave a yawning view over the Peak countryside, even from the centre of town. I could see the weaving, waving hills and dales, delineated here and there into farmer's fields by hedgerows and low stone walls. The morning mist had yet to completely burn away from the deeps, where it slowly swirled like stirred milk.

Above me was the castle, casting its craggy shadow on the town. As I approached, the path and hill narrowed, falling away on my right to pasture and to the left another cobbled road leading to a stone church and unkempt graveyard. On the arch of the wrought-iron cemetery gate a crow perched and issued me an ominous 'caw!' in that tone crows use to express that they know something you don't.

Up close, the castle was only more intimidating, like a dowager aunt, sitting in the corner at a wedding, holding the purse strings. It had been constructed initially of black gritstone and repaired over the ages with uncut granite, cement, whole tree trunks, and what looked like the running board of a 1921 Vauxhall E-Type. The massive portcullis — large enough to permit three horses to trot through without so much as acknowledging each other, had a smaller, human-sized door cut into it, complete with a heavy, iron knocker in the shape of some horned demon with a ring in its jaws and a certain apotropaic quality, like a gargoyle, only less hospitable.

The door screeched slowly open and, sure enough, there stood the head butler from the Castle Pub last night.

"What ho, old tipplemate," I said, stepping into the mediaeval interior. The gatehouse of the castle was one of those grand unheatable stone caverns that generate their own sources of cold and damp, lit by flaming torches on granite columns that reach to one another across a high, vaulted ceiling.

"Good morning, sir," said Head Butler Carnaby. He was much improved on the day, as though having spent the night in a much dryer ditch and taken the time to shave in the dark.

"I've come on your sage advice, Carnaby, hunting Wurts. Got any on hand?"

"That'd be me, sir. I'm Wurt."

"You are?"

"That's right. Wurt Carnaby, at your service."

"But last night you told me that the only W Carnaby on staff at the castle was called Wurt. Is there, against all odds, a second Wurt?"

"No, sir. I was referring to myself."

"I see," I claimed. "Minor point of order — why didn't you mention it?"

"Well, you didn't ask, did you?"

"I daresay you're right, reflecting back on the spirited exchange of ideas that was our evening, I didn't. Must have overlooked it."

Temporarily in check, I put my hands behind my back and wandered the great hall. It was a fully grown gatehouse, about the size of a modest cathedral at the back of which immense lancet windows, a good two London stories high, filtered grey morning light through dusty panes. Tattered tapestries hung on the walls between the columns and pursued one another up the wide stone staircase that disappeared into darkness.

"On a hunch, Wurt old man, are there any other W Carnabys on hand?" I asked.

"There's Wselfwulf Carnaby." Wurt pronounced this as though it may well have begun with a W or, for that matter, an epsilon, which was in any case silent. Sort of a 'Sethworth' sound, spoken by a lifelong drinker.

"Stout, solid sort of chap? Red of cheek and floppy of ear? Exudes duty and decorum from all pores simultaneously?"

"Could be."

"Recently arrived from London, then?"

"Mister Wselfwulf came up from London about two weeks ago."

"That's the chap," I said, drawing my calling card. "Could you tell him that Anthony Boisjoly craves audience."

Wurt took the card and shuffled toward and then beyond the stairs. I heard doors opening and closing and then Wurt returned, followed by the W Carnaby I know from the Juniper.

"Mister Anthony Boisjoly," announced Wurt.

"What ho, Carnaby. I came to find out what the W in your name stands for and may I say, I'm very glad I did."

Carnaby maintained a stunned half-smile and divided a nervous glance between myself and Wurt, and then said the very last thing I expected to hear from London's finest club steward.

"Anty old chap, how splendid to see you."

CHAPTER THREE

Riches Which Pitch Witches into Deep Ditches

"I do beg your pardon, Mister Boisjoly." Carnaby had led me to a comparatively small drawing room the rough size and dimensions of the international lounge at Victoria Station. We sat across from each other on overstuffed settées before a largely symbolic fire and surrounded by bookshelves and paintings and the glimmering knickknacks of five hundred years of hoarding.

"Think nothing of it, Carnaby," I said. "The pub landlord explained to me the decidedly binary class system of the town. You're a Castle Carnaby, I take it, and it would be awkward if it were known that you were in service in London."

"You understand entirely."

"And you let it be understood that you're a member of the Juniper, providing a posh address at which you can be reached in London."

"It seemed a judicious dissimulation."

"And reach you someone did." I withdrew the telegram from my breast pocket. "You had us worried. Hallowit pines for the anonymity of the role of second barman."

"Indeed. It was this telegram which drew me to Hoy. I had planned to spend my holiday studying new developments in brandy chafing at *l'école Escoffier.*"

"I've seen you in action, Carnaby, and assumed that you held some sort of DSc."

"It's a living art, sir," said Carnaby with light reproach. "No one is ever an expert."

"And you gave that a miss for a chance to be carried off by a curse." I held up the telegram for reference.

"The Carnaby Castle Curse has never claimed a male victim, Mister Boisjoly," explained Carnaby. "I don't believe that the message was a threat toward me, or even a threat. It was a warning that, were I to come, I would be met with the death of someone else."

"And your notorious sense of duty brought you rushing toward danger," I said. "Like that time you put yourself bodily between Lord Snowsill-Willit and that bee that had found its way into the dining hall."

"An apt comparison, sir," said Carnaby. "I received the telegram as a call to action."

"Any idea who sent it?" I again studied the postmark, which revealed nothing less sensational than the revelation that Chesterfield has a post office with telegraph capabilities.

"None at all. I asked Wurt if he had been sent to the post office in Chesterfield at some point prior to my arrival, and he was only able to confirm that it was possible."

I had, in the moment, one of those cold surmises, as when one is walking down the street, chatting animatedly with an old chum, when one realises that one has been walking shoulder-to-shoulder with a total stranger. It was something Carnaby had said moments before — something about male victims of the curse and calls to action. I went quickly over my mental notes, and then it came to me.

"I say, Carnaby, you're not saying you believe all this tosh about curses."

"Oh, it's all true, Mister Boisjoly." Carnaby ceased pacing to focus on me the wide, staring eyes of the faithful. "I've seen it myself."

"Did you, Carnaby? What form did it take? Locusts?"

"Mists, Mister Boisjoly. I watched them carry away Ludovica, Cecil Carnaby's wife."

"I understood that she'd been shoved over the cliff."

"Swept over, is how I'd put it." Carnaby nodded approval of his own appraisal.

"Swept over, then," I conceded. "Why?"

"I beg your pardon?"

"Why?" I asked again. "Why did the curse want to do any sweeping at all, never mind that of a perfectly innocent young bride?"

"I don't know that she was so innocent as all that, Mister Boisjoly," said Carnaby vaguely. "However, she was selected by the curse exactly because she's a young bride."

"Rather grimly specific criteria," I opined. "What interest does the curse have in one's marital status?"

"It's how it all began, sir, about four hundred years ago. The feudal lord of the time, Ranulf Carnaby, brought the curse down upon the castle when he cheated a local witch, who had done him a service."

"Always a mistake," I advised. "My father forgot so many merchants' cuffs in his time that for years I believed Christmas porridge to be a Boisjoly family tradition."

"This instance might be considered worse. Certainly more enduring. Ranulf had engaged a witch with respect to the pressing problem of an heir — he and his wife, Matilde, were childless, and approaching an age after which it became increasingly less likely that she would ever bear him a son. Witches at the time were commonly consulted on such matters, such as a disappointing crop yield or late spring thaw."

"Or a drought in the family hatchery."

"Colourfuly stated, but yes, sir, as in the case of Ranulf, he asked a witch recorded as Ravena Sooter to intervene. She agreed to do so, conditional that on the birth of his son she would be accorded title to a small portion of the lands comprising his fief. He agreed."

"But weaselled."

"History suggests that he had cause," explained Carnaby. "You see, that winter, without bearing him a son, Matilde died."

"At the risk of stealing your punchline, Carnaby, did she die in a fall?"

Carnaby nodded gravely. "She had been walking on the promontory above Hoy Scarp when, according to contemporary accounts, the mists rose from the river, raised her in the air, and flung her into the gorge."

"Seems a fairly clear case of breach of contract. So far the court of public opinion is siding with Ranulf."

"It doesn't end there, though," continued Carnaby. "A year later, Ranulf married a girl from the village — the daughter of a vassal — and shortly thereafter she bore him a son."

"Ah."

"Indeed, sir. On the day of the boy's birth, Ravena Sooter appeared, demanding payment and taking credit for the birth of an heir and, by extension, responsibility for the death of Matilde."

"Technically delivering on the agreement, but with a textbook Monkey's Paw clause," I observed.

"Ranulf took exception. Not only did he not honour the agreement, he put Ravena Sooter on trial for witchcraft, and began a campaign of persecution of her kind within his area of influence."

"Must have made it a little challenging finding a jury of her peers," I pointed out.

"In fact Ravena Sooter was given trial by ordeal."

"One of those, damned if you do, dead if you don't, sort of affairs?"

"Precisely, sir," said Carnaby. "Ravena Sooter was thrown from Hoy Scarp, at the same point from which Matilde Carnaby was fetched up by the mists. It was presumed that, if she were indeed a witch, the mists would save her."

22

"I'm going to leap ahead and assume that the mists did not, in fact, save her," I leapt. "At least they all learned something from the experience."

"On the contrary, sir."

"What? You're not telling me the mists came to the rescue of Ravena Sooter."

"No, but in her final moments she confessed all, and placed a curse on Carnaby Castle and, more specifically, any young bride who might bring it an heir."

"You know, whatever else you might think of witches — one might easily differ on the eye of newt question and the whole pointy hat business — you have to admire their sense of irony."

"The measure was indeed very effective," agreed Carnaby. "As young Carnabys married and tragedy inevitably struck, the family soon dissipated. Anyone wishing to raise a family would move to the village, and sometimes further afield. Enough would occasionally return to lay claim to the castle that it remained in the Carnaby name, but this led as often as not to deadly dispute. Eventually the two distinct family lines formed — the Castle Carnabys and the Town Carnabys."

"Well that brings us neatly up to Cecil Carnaby and his young bride, Ludovica, if memory serves," I summarised. "What made the happy couple ready to face down the combined forces of superstition and twaddle?"

"Cecil Carnaby, I believe, shares your Cartesian view of the curse. In any case, he had been abroad for many years — he's something of the prodigal son of the family — and only returned to Hoy on Monday. Furthermore, he and Ludovica had already been married, some six weeks earlier, in Italy."

"But the curse saw through that naked ploy."

"Manifestly so."

"Well, Carnaby." I stood, now, to be eye-to-eye with my club steward. "Whether or not you or I or anyone else believes in the Carnaby Castle Curse, I can assure you that Scotland Yard will not."

"Yes, in fact, we've had an Inspector Wittersham at the castle all morning." Carnaby said this with a sort of mystified air, as though he had yet to make the connection between a suspicious death and the appearance of a police officer.

"I know the man," I said. "And I can assure you that he won't leave without an earthly explanation for what happened to Ludovica Carnaby and, ideally, someone sufficiently temporal to instruct defence counsel."

"I feel confident there's nothing to be concerned about, Mister Boisjoly," said Carnaby, expressing an endearing naivety not typically displayed by your cynical, world-weary club steward.

"Nevertheless, Carnaby, it's essential that I be on hand, if only to defend your interests," I said. "You may not be aware, but there are those in my modest circle who have often relied upon me to restore order where once chaos reigned."

"Oh, yes, indeed Mister Boisjoly. Your accomplishments are the subject of much discussion among the staff at the Juniper, if you'll pardon the liberty."

"You know all about that little drama in Fray last year then."

"Very much so, yes, and the extraordinary Christmas you passed in Hertfordshire, and of course that unfortunate situation involving Mister Tenpenny."

"Oh, right." I was unused to not accounting for myself. I felt very much how I imagine bit players feel when another actor pinches their only line. "It's not always life or death, you understand, for instance, you probably didn't hear about the confidential service I provided fellow Juniper Cribbage Digby…"

"If you're referring to the occasion on which you appeared in court as Mister Digby to answer a charge of driving a hansom cab through Burlington Arcade, your altruism in that instance is much esteemed below stairs."

"It was nothing, really," I said with a dismissive wave. "Goes some distance in atoning for all the times I wasn't caught."

"And we recently learned of the timely assistance you provided Lord Hannibal-Pool when Lady Hannibal-Pool suspected him of going off his diet."

"Modesty protests a bit at that one — I merely sourced a doctor willing to write a prescription for butterscotch. Pure luck her ladyship never asked if he was a medical doctor or a PhD in Indo-European languages."

"Of course any assistance you can offer would be very much appreciated, Mister Boisjoly, but Inspector Wittersham will eventually have to accept that Ludovica was claimed by the curse — no human could possibly have done it.

❦

When I returned to the Castle Pub and Inn, Ivor and Blewit were at a corner table, speaking in low tones over high tea, or at any rate a sumptuous clutter of beef and Buxton blue pie, buns, bread, butter, and brimming pints of bitter.

"What ho, fellow students of the human condition," I said, pulling a stool up to the trough. "I had Local Lore and Legends this morning with Professor Carnaby, what did you have?"

Their beef-and-buxton-blue-pie-holes otherwise occupied, the policemen greeted me with a silent toast performed in beer.

"Would that be your club steward?" asked Ivor, finally.

"It would," I said in hushed tones. "But that's not meant to get about. Apparently the Castle Carnabys are a class-conscious clan, so as far as anyone's concerned he's a London man of leisure."

"One of those moneyed idlers, flitting between club and theatre, and making no real contribution apart from paying the occasional fine levied for public drunkenness?" speculated Ivor.

"Oh, very subtle, Inspector," I said. "But yes, in fact, he appears to have very much modelled his London legend on the Boisjoly before you. Talking of legends, he also gave me the newsreel version of the origins of the Carnaby Castle Curse. Care to hear them?"

"Not particularly," said Ivor. "I think we've gathered the fundamentals from witness statements."

"Is everyone, like my own country-bred Carnaby, convinced that Ludovica Carnaby was claimed by a four-hundred-year-old curse?"

"Not everyone." Ivor cast an eye toward Blewit, who replied with a guileless smile. "You should know, Constable, that Mister Boisjoly has been quite helpful in previous cases. He has something of a gift for aggravating out the truth."

"I understand, sir."

"And so, Inspector," I said, picking up the thread, "you were about to tell me that the only person interviewed who remains unswayed by the curse theory is the victim's husband, Cecil Carnaby."

"Already spoken to them, have you?"

"I have not, in fact," I replied, while improvising a sandwich of crusty bread, crumbly cheddar, and crispy pickle. "But I will do. I've secured lodgings at the castle. I've only come back to rescue my affairs from the attic. Carnaby assures me, though, that no human force could have done the terrible deed."

"That appears to be the broad consensus among the witnesses," agreed Ivor. "Constable?"

Blewit, sensing a great famine approaching, pushed a knob of pie into his mouth before setting aside his plate and replacing it with a handsomely worn notebook.

"Friday evening, around dusk, six members of the household and staff were witness to the death of Mrs Ludovica Carnaby... formerly Mrs Trewsbury-Birkit. These witnesses are Mrs Elisabeth Stokely..." Blewit looked up from his reading to add, "née Carnaby... was in her room in the north tower. Barnaby and Cressida Carnaby were on the allure — the walkway atop the north wall."

"There's a Barnaby Carnaby?" I asked, obviously, delighted.

"Mister Barnaby and Miss Cressida are the nephew and niece of Mrs Stokely."

"Right-oh."

"Mister Wselfwulf Carnaby, cousin to Cecil Carnaby and Elisabeth Stokely, was in the library in the keep, looking out the window."

"Is the view to the north of the castle particularly breathtaking at that time of the evening?" I asked. "Is that corner of the sky renowned for shooting stars? Does the sun, in this magical part of the kingdom, set in the north? Rather a coincidence, if not, that everyone was looking the same direction at the same time."

"We noticed that, too," said Ivor. "One rather receives the impression that the household was suspicious of the new bride, and tended to keep an eye on her."

"Finally," concluded Blewit, "three members of staff — Miss Prax Carnaby, Miss Lindingfleis Carnaby, and Mister Wurt Carnaby — were performing their duties in the kitchen and main house respectively, and they, too, happened to be looking toward the scarp when they saw Mrs Ludovica, in their words, fetched up."

"And what did that entail?"

"There's a river at the bottom of a sharp cliff where Hoy Tor ends on the north side. It's not uncommon for thick mists to rise from these rivers, and such was the case Friday night, to hear tell it. As our eyewitnesses watched, one such mist rolled over the edge of the scarp, where Mrs Ludovica was walking, and enveloped her. An instant later, she was gone. Some confusion followed as stories were compared — people not believing their eyes, they say — and a party was sent to the scarp. Below them, on the rocks, was the body of the deceased."

"The mists enveloped her?" I pursued this notable point. "There you have it, then — in that moment someone leapt from a clever hiding spot, chucked her over, and leapt back to the aforementioned clever hiding spot. Probably a bush. Were there any hollow trees to hand?"

"Nothing of the sort, really," said Ivor, spoiling things as usual. "Furthermore the ground was damp, and Ludovica's footprints were evident. There were no others."

"Oh, do come along, Inspector."

"Just giving you the facts, Boisjoly. We've seen stranger things."

"Could she have jumped?"

"By all accounts the lady was very happy — young, pretty, newly married into a wealthy family…" countered Blewit.

"Possibly a student of statesman and philosopher Solon — *'Count no man happy until the end is known'* — having levelled up in life, she decides to bank her winnings in a single, bold gesture."

"In her room I found a letter to her mother, bound for the post, describing in happy terms the details of her life at the castle." Blewit once again put me in check.

"I don't suppose she might have just tripped."

"There is a substantial wooden barrier."

"Of course there is." I distracted myself briefly with a bit of the sort of cheddar one can only get in London if one has connections in high office. "You've missed one, I think — where was Cecil Carnaby?"

"Mister Cecil was not in the castle at the time," said Blewit. "He was in the village. Visiting the cemetery, to be precise. Says he was collecting material for his memoir."

"I trust everyone can back up their claims."

"Very nearly." Ivor took over the offensive. "Barnaby and Cressida were together. The maid found the butler and Mrs Stokely, who had been in her room in the north tower, in the courtyard. This is also true of the cook, Prax Carnaby, who had been in the south tower. There were no other parties in or near the castle."

"Except…"

"Yes," confirmed Ivor. "The only one without an alibi is your steward, Carnaby."

CHAPTER FOUR

A Peek at the Peaks of Peak From a Peaky Peak

Vickers, it turned out, was not at home. I packed my own bag and checked in with Odd, who reported that Vickers had gone out for a constitutional sometime after breakfast and hadn't been seen since.

Vickers has moments during which he can get lost on his way to sleep, so I wrapped further provisions from the policemen's feast in my handkerchief, in case he'd fallen down a well or become irretrievably trapped in a revolving door, and went exploring.

I hadn't far to go. The other road I'd seen on first arriving in Hoy was, in fact, the only other road in town. It was much like the first, except that on the one side it was stone cottages and a small but scary church formed of weathered granite blocks and ornamented with judgemental grotesques, and on the other side a cemetery. The graveyard was enclosed by a low wall of whole rocks and it had the worn, overgrown, irresistible charm of an ancestor repository in continuous use across the centuries. It was mainly weather-beaten tombstones and thin mausoleums, like a town of tiny basilicas, and at the centre was what appeared to be the entrance to a catacomb. A low, dense fog flowed slowly between the gravestones.

And the street was deserted, with the exception of, on the wrought-iron arch above the cemetery lichgate where I'd first seen him, a crow, who presently greeted me with a friendly 'caw' that somehow sounded like a question.

"As you've asked," I said to the bird, who cocked his head and displayed a unique white patch above his left eye, "I'm looking for my man, Vickers. Haven't seen him have you? About my height, indeterminate age, may or may not be wearing trousers."

The crow replied with a 'could be, let me think' sort of cackle, then took flight across the road and settled on a wooden sign, swinging from an iron bar and marking out one of the cottages as another pub. Interestingly, the name on the sign was, of all things, the Castle, and the mystery was almost certainly solved.

"Ta very kindly," I said to the crow. I selected a bun from among the provisions and placed it on the gatepost outside the pub. The crow fluttered down to it, gave me a furtive but friendly nod, and set about dismantling the bun.

The interior of the second Castle Pub was a shiny mirror of the first. They were both laid out in a distinctly and not-entirely-unexpected pub-like fashion, with a bartop beneath hanging glassware, stools with pudgy cushions and low tables, and chattering patrons. But this Castle Pub was polished and pleasant and permeated with natural light from large windows at the front and back. The feminine touch, one might say, and indeed the theme extended to the barman, who was in fact a barmaid — a statuesque contrast of pale skin and long black hair, polishing a copper tankard.

As forecast by the crow, Vickers was there. He shared a back window table with a broad, beefy bloke in city livery of a pinstriped suit and French cuffs. I organised a short ale from the bar and joined them.

"As you are, Vickers," I said, relieving him of the effort of leaping nimbly to his feet. I occupied the upholstered cast-iron window seat.

"Good afternoon, Mister Boisjoly." Vickers appeared about as comfortable as a lifelong valet can when trapped into egalitarian society with his employer. He had the tortured countenance of a member of the court of Tzar Nicholas accidentally finding himself at a Bolshevik tea party. "May I present Elwin Jones. Mister Jones, Mister Anthony Boisjoly."

"Call me Anty," I said, "and join the league of millions."

"Call me Win," said Elwin, sort of possessing the table and glaring at me beneath brilliantined and marcelled hair like a damp mountain road and a brow like a leg of lamb, "'cause I always do."

"You always call yourself Win?" I asked.

"No, I mean, well, yes."

"Right oh. Somewhat circular reasoning, to my mind, but who am I to judge. What brings you to Hoy, Win?"

"What makes you think I'm not from here?"

"Are you?"

"No." Win leaned back with his pint. "Ancestry."

"Anty," I gently corrected.

"No, I mean I'm researching my ancestry. I believe that my people may be from Hoy."

"Well, many people are," I confirmed. "I understand that dating back to sometime in the fifth century being from Hoy was all the rage."

Win looked disparagingly about the pub. "'Bout all there is to do around here. Ever done any whitewater canoeing, Anty?"

"I rowed at Oxford."

"What about mountain climbing?"

"Not as such, no," I reflected. "Headington Hill can get a bit steepish after a large evening."

"Pah!" Win waved dismissively. "Eaten rattlesnake? Broken a wild horse?"

"Are those related activities?" I asked. "I once broke a valuable porcelain elephant. Do you remember that Vickers? Hideous thing."

"What are you two doing here, anyway?"

31

"Well, in point of fact, our remit has rather evolved since making landfall," I answered. "Moral support, now, I suppose. There's been a family tragedy up at the castle."

"Oh yes? Who died? One of those, what do they call them, Castle Carnabys?"

"I don't know that I'm at liberty to say," I said coolly, "but yes, one of those, what do you call them, Castle Carnabys."

"None of my business I don't suppose." Win drained his pint in a single throw, banged down his tankard like the gavel of a hanging judge, and rushed to his feet. "If I'm a Carnaby, I'm a towny. Pleasure meeting you, Anty, Mister Vickers." And he strode out the door.

"Have I ever eaten rattlesnake, Vickers?"

"The Boisjoly kitchen has long practised a decidedly hidebound policy with respect to reptiles."

"How did you come to make the acquaintance of the adventurous Mister Jones? Did you discover a mutual interest in chivvying wild horses?"

"I was reconnoitring the village, sir, in respect of your instruction to become acquainted with the town and its inhabitants," said Vickers. "I found myself disoriented, at some point, and asked him to direct me to the Castle Pub."

"At the risk of sounding pedantic," I differed, "you asked him to direct you to *a* castle pub. Turns out there are two of them."

Vickers looked slowly around the room, settling his gaze finally on the barmaid.

"How extraordinary."

"Isn't it?" I agreed. "You'd think a town of this size wouldn't have run out of names for its pubs so quickly."

"I wonder if the escutcheon might partially explain the anomaly." Vickers was still studying the bar and I followed his eyes to a shield mounted above it with a coat of arms — castle argent on field gules, atop hill slightly dodgy — doubtless the crest of the current Castle Carnaby.

"I see what you mean," I said. "One of those partisan arrangements, like the Star and Garter in Oxford and its namesake in Lancashire, which bar entry to all and the descendants of all who've ever played cricket for either university, respectively."

"Can such a thing be enforced?" asked Vickers.

"One can just tell." Denied the luxury of a first-class education, Vickers can be forgiven for not knowing this. "But if this is the Castle Carnaby pub, what was a towny like Elwin Jones doing here?"

"I would note, sir, that this is not the most curious aspect of the character of Mister Jones," said Vickers. "For instance, his name is not Jones."

"Isn't it? How do you come to know that?"

"I chanced to observe that he was wearing cufflinks monogrammed with the initials S.T."

"Odd — and highly dubious from a haberdashery perspective — but hardly conclusive."

"Furthermore, when I introduced him to you as Elwin Jones, I had briefly forgotten that he had introduced himself to me as Elwin Smith."

"Yes, that does seem like the sort of thing one would pick up on," I agreed. "Well, in fact that brings us nicely to what I'm calling phase two of the plan I just formed. I'm moving to the castle, Vickers, but I need you to remain here in the village. You must be my eyes and ears and, with particular regard to the cheddar, my palate."

"Very good, sir."

"First thing you'll want to do, once we chart a course back to base, is to recount your encounter with the mysterious Smith-Jones to Inspector Wittersham," I said. "Poor chap is suffering an embarrassing shortage of suspects, and for the moment is concentrating his conclusion-leaping skills on Carnaby the club steward."

Built and improved more in keeping with the vicissitudes visited upon it during the War of the Barons than for, say, comfort, Carnaby Castle had something of the warm, domestic charm of a breakwater prison.

It wasn't even a single thing really, but a crumbling chaos of towers and turrets and tumbling battlements, raised and razed and rebuilt and ruined over a thousand years of bickering neighbours. The north and south towers appeared to be so called because they were, in fact, the north and south *intact* towers. The other habitable structures included the gatehouse and a barbican at the front and back, a sizable keep, and a sort of main house built into the rear wall.

Wurt walked me into the courtyard and to the southwest corner and the entrance to the tower.

"Yours is the second floor, Mister Boisjoly." Wurt opened the wooden door at the base of the tower and handed me a key. "I won't accompany you, if you'll permit, sir. I can't manage the stairs in my condition."

"Condition, Wurt?" I expressed my feudal concern. "What condition is that?"

"I'm stewed, sir," he answered plainly. "It often comes upon me at this time of day. Only gets worse with the approach of evening."

"Oh, right. For what it's worth, I'll tell you what I often do when I need to combat those symptoms."

"I wish you would, sir."

"On such occasions — and they're rare enough — I don't drink. Or at any rate not before at least one bell of cocktail rings."

"Ah, no, sir." Wurt shook his head sadly, as one soldiering on beneath the amassed weight of an unjust fate. "I'm afraid that would never take."

"Cut back a little then?"

"All avenues have been explored." Wurt illustrated the point with a flask deftly withdrawn from the breast pocket, uncorked, and made good use of.

"I say, Wurt, can't think of what makes me think of it, but do I understand that you were an eyewitness to the unfortunate end met by Mrs Ludovica Carnaby?"

Wurt's eyes widened and held mine with an unnerving intensity.

"Taken up by the mists, she was."

"Yes, it's this very point on which I hoped to take your mind," I said. "Are you quite certain of what you saw?"

"Not at all, sir." Wurt shook his head with concrete conviction. "I assumed, in fact, that it was a delirium, to which I am often prey."

"But you've since been reassured."

"Indeed, sir. I saw it from the main house." Wurt gestured with his bulbous nose toward the solid rectangular building built into the back wall, about the size and shape of a residential block in Chelsea. "I come down to the kitchen and the maid, who was boiling the sheets at the time, told me she seen the same thing I did."

"Did you happen to meet anyone else along the way?"

"Only Mrs Stokely. She was going the other way, with a view to locking herself in the keep, as a precaution, you see, against the curse coming for her next."

"Is that standard practice? I would have thought that mist, by its very nature, would have had rather the run of the place."

Wurt nodded in sage agreement and then, with a start, appeared to recall that he had duties elsewhere.

"Dinner's at eight, Mister Boisjoly," he said, lurching back toward the gatehouse. "Dining room is in the main house. There's no bell."

The south tower was dark and damp. Kerosene railway lamps lit the winding staircase, which otherwise rose above me into the blackness. At what my knees felt — and I agreed — was well far enough for a second floor I finally arrived at a door, but it was bolted from the this side. Nevertheless, I threw the bolt and opened the door and found myself looking at the windswept allure — a walkway the full immense width of the wall, defended on the external side by crumbling ramparts. It led from my tower to the west wall, and thence to the north wall and tower. Beyond that, presumably, was Hoy Scarp and the belligerent fog.

I bolted the door and continued to the second floor, which turned out to be a creaky wooden platform and an ancient door of oak and iron. Home.

My room was a casual clutter of the comforts of a mediaeval fortress richly enhanced with the shoddiness of modern renovation techniques. It was also a long-term victim of the decorating custom, practised in great houses across the land, which dictates that all unused and/or unsightly art and artefacts are stored in the spare guest room. The walls were an eclectic clutter of paintings, shields, oars, swords, and spears, and the floor was a lumpy landscape of the hides of several unfortunate bears. The bed was a musty four-poster that was simultaneously too big and too small. From above the high, cold, whistling fireplace, the head of a poorly taxidermied boar stared straight ahead, as though musing on a short life of poor decisions.

What had doubtless once been a convenient lookout from which to dish generous servings of boiling oil to anyone who came calling had been converted into a high Juliet balcony. It gave me vertigo just looking at it from the other side of the room, but the curtain was held with a stout length of chain. I took hold of the chain and stepped into the shrieking wind.

I was immediately rewarded with a not-insignificant measure of a full-scale map of the Peak District. Beneath me the village

36

rolled down two meandering roads. A river, which bordered the cemetery, bubbled beneath a stone bridge, bustled along the waterwheel of a working mill, and broadened a bit before babbling with an acquaintance at the bottom of Hoy Hill. The river would have come from the other side of the hill and at some point in the past several million years must have been instrumental in forming it.

The Peak District, clearly, is where everything started. The story of the formation of the planet — or at any rate the nicer bits — is carved here in sharp relief. Great columns of ancient rock are pushed out of the earth's crust as though by an explosive, subterranean laboratory experiment somehow gone right. Folds and rolls of plump hill are scooped out of lush green valleys to gently plop into their most natural and obvious of place, only to have jagged chunks bitten out of their backs by faults which spill away over the millenia to form eccentric tumbles of cliffy parks and iffy scarps. Anyone keeping an eye on the place over the last million years or so would have had no idea what all this chaos was in aid of — rushing seas and crushing ice and gushing volcanos operating with, at best, independent agendas, could reasonably be expected to produce a disordered, even Hebridean landscape.

But now it's all tamed, or at least becalmed. Now it's dips of downy mist and highs of walkable tips and smooth, soft meadow, pasture, field, farm, river and stream flowing in between.

We're here by kind consent of countryside, and we're represented by sheep, mainly, and distant steeples and stumbling hedgerows, stacked stone walls, and winding roads that weave by comfortable accommodation of hill and valley.

My eyes meandered along the road back to Hoy, now charmingly backlit by a setting sun that sliced into spotlights on the cemetery. With the light and the distance and the wind and the feral fear of heights it was difficult to focus on the two figures appearing from the shadows of the catacombs and a crypt — both tall, certainly, and surreptitious and draped in black.

The whipping wind had watered my eyes to a blur. I blinked away the blear and when I looked again a black and furtive figure had become a fluttering, screeching black wraith careening toward me from the graveyard. I made a quick, preliminary peace with the hereafter and, as an added precaution, yelped like a Pekingese. Buffeted by the wind, the trajectory of the thing was like a drunken scrum-half, and it dropped briefly from view before returning as the neighbourhood cemetery crow. He landed on the rampart, was immediately blown away, and flapped about once again out of sight. I leaned forward as far as my curtain chain would allow but could see nothing until, in a clamorous chaos of wing and wind, he tumbled over the rampart and onto the balcony.

"What ho, old crow," I said, but he was still looking resentfully at the elements. "Let us talk inside, where we won't be disturbed."

I pulled myself back into the room by my chain and the crow followed, stalking in that awkwardly determined, straight-legged fashion of his species. He hopped up onto a threadbare Bergère chair and I gave him the last bun from my reserves.

"I only just arrived myself, and I'm afraid that's all I have to offer guests, Crow old thing."

The crow seemed very content with the bun, however, which he held down by foot and got stuck into by beak.

"Can't very well go on calling you Crow, can I?" I said. "You should have a name that evokes the sleek, supernatural spirit of the night-black harbinger of dark tidings from the netherworld. How about... Buns?" Buns cocked his head as though considering the motion, then returned to his tea. "There's a Buns Peabody at the Juniper, but I doubt very much he'll mind. I may not even tell him."

A subtle, almost subliminal tick, like the little preparatory 'ahem' that alarm clocks emit just before losing their minds, drew our attention. Buns spotted the source instantly and said something that sounded very like 'clawk' and, in the next instant, the elaborately ugly coach clock on the mantelpiece dinged eight times.

"Right you are, Buns." I set about a quick and cursory dress for dinner. "Time to meet the suspects."

CHAPTER FIVE

The Brisk Business of Being Boisjoly

I knew who everyone was before introductions, as though I'd read the cast list in the programme. Brooding at the head of the table, like Orpheus grieving Eurydice before picking up and going to Hades to get her back, was what must have been Cecil Carnaby, darkly isolated in misery for Ludovica. He was trimly turned out in a dinner jacket that had been fitted for him when his shoulders were less broad, and he had greying sideburns and a granite jaw and angry, angry eyebrows. To his right and facing me when I entered the mediaeval dining room with a tiny fire in a massive inglenook, was a woman of roughly the same middle-age as Cecil, with steel-grey hair tied severely back, as though for optimal aerodynamics, a doughy, distant sort of expression, and high eyebrows that, as Mrs Elisabeth Stokely saw me, seemed to say 'who is this person, and why has he come to kill me?' Next to her was Carnaby, exhibiting the same level and lot of discomfort that I'd seen on Vickers' face earlier that day when he was obliged to share a table in a pub with his employer.

I observed Carnaby quietly resisting the urge to stand. Instead he only smiled and said "Ah, Boisjoly, finally made it." And this caused what were doubtless Barnaby and Cressida Carnaby to turn and appraise the new arrival. Barnaby Carnaby was a thin, pop-eyed chap of about my age, with untamed curly hair and a poorly tailored dinner jacket. Cressida had blonde, viscous hair and she, too, was thin in a reedy sort of way accentuated by a willowy frock with as many too many sequins for the occasion as would fit.

"What ho, Mister Boisjoly," called Barnaby. "Pip-pip, and all that."

"Good evening, Mister Boisjoly." Cressida spoke in a breathy drawl that I expect was meant as beguiling but instead came across as slightly asthmatic. "How delightful to have the company of a diverting newcomer."

Carnaby made introductions and I was four for four in the first innings until a handsome woman with a wise and wizened face came in by the service door. Prax Carnaby, was my guess, castle cook. She looked about the same age as Elizabeth Stokely and Cecil, but wore it more comfortably, as she did her laundry-softened cook's frock and apron, and the satisfied smile that she derived from hovering over the consommé bubbling in a cauldron above the fire.

Prax was followed by what was either the most slovenly maid I've ever seen or an animated stack of unwashed laundry. She was very nearly my height and at her thickest point about the circumference of my left arm at its thinnest. She wore an off-white pinafore with a broken strap and an exciting assortment of stains and fuzz. Her Carnaby-brown hair looked to have been arranged by some free-spirited nesting bird with little interest in settling down.

"Lint," is apparently what Prax called the maid, "you may begin serving the soup." That would make this Lindingfleis Carnaby who listlessly took charge of the tureen and splashed a clear broth into our dishes.

Beneath the cover of clinking cutlery and sloshing soup, Mrs Stokely evidently thought she discreetly whispered to Carnaby, "Who is this new person? I don't like his looks one bit."

Carnaby smiled that awkward smile with which I will ever associate his castle identity.

"Anthony knows there's always an open invitation for him here, Bunty."

"Anty, if you like," I offered, hoping that Bunty and I might find common ground on the theme of diminutives. Instead, she pursed her lips and looked at me askance and took a very quick but meaningful inventory of her jewellery, which included a memorably hideous bauble — possibly some sort of flying insect preserved in amber — hanging round her neck.

"How's the metropolis these days, Anty?" Barnaby introduced a welcome lighter tone. "Feels like weeks since I've been down."

"Weeks, Nobby?" laughed Cressida.

"Yes, thank you, Sid. It has been weeks. Several," said Barnaby cooly. "Seen anything good lately?"

"Oh, rather." I had to set down my spoon and focus, nobbled, as I was, without my theatre programmes and ticket stubs and souvenir sheet music to remind me what I'd seen. "Obviously the hit of the season is the revival of Coward's *Bittersweet* at the Palace — enormous cast, real gunfire and a miraculous scene-change to Vienna and back. Put me in a mood, don't you know, so, same night, I saw *The Five O'Clock Girl* at the Hippodrome. Seen it?"

"Uhm, let me think…" Barnaby searched the skies. "No, not yet."

"Absolute corker. No idea what it was about. Something regarding a girl and five o'clock, I expect. Two acts, just a shade under ninety minutes and yet, somehow, over three hours of libretto. When they pushed us out into the street a policeman asked me my business and all I could think of was the lyrics to *I'm One Little Party.*"

"I must make a note to see it when I'm next down."

"It's closed, I'm afraid. Been replaced by *Hit the Deck*. Bit samey throughout, if you take my meaning, but that's rather to be expected with your naval themed musicals — all *Join the Navy* and *Shore Leave* and, if you will, *Harbour of My Heart* — what you want to see is *Wake Up and Dream* at the Pavillion. This Cole Porter chappy has a future, you can tell anyone I said so."

"Have you seen *Lady be Good* at the Empire?" asked Barnaby, casually.

"Sadly, no," I said. "They turned the Empire into a cinema."

"Oh, dear. When did that happen?"

"1927," I replied.

"Ha!" barked Cressida. "My brother thinks of himself as a Londoner playing the role of an oppressed provincial, which is true, except exactly the other way 'round."

"And my sister," countered Barnaby, "thinks of herself as my oppressor, which is also true, full-stop."

"Are you like Wselfwulf, Anty?" asked Cressida.

"How much now?"

"Uncle Wselfwulf," elaborated Cressida, providing me a vital instant to translate 'Wselfwulf' to 'Carnaby'. "I understand that you belong to the same club, so I wondered if you were also one of the luxuriously idle rich."

This was spoken in something of the tone of an appraisal, as one sizing up a chap as he hung by his feet in a butcher's window.

"Perhaps not so idle as all that." In the moment and since I have no idea why I felt the need to show well. Some guileless instinct, I expect. "Possibly Carnaby, or Wselfwulf, as you prefer, told you of the peculiar circumstances around what the papers came to call the Tale of the Tenpenny Tontine."

"Indeed he did," confirmed Barnaby.

"The police were utterly baffled," I continued. "Well, not so much baffled as initially uninterested, but it took some post-graduate level sleuthing, I can tell you that. Did Wselfwulf happen to mention the case of the Canterfell Codicil, which concerned the murder — behind locked doors, mind — of the uncle of our fellow clubman Fiddles Canterfell?"

"Yes," gushed Cressida, "Uncle Wselfwulf told us that the police didn't even suspect there was a second murder until he pointed out the clue of the pigeons."

"Uncle Wselfwulf? Pigeons?" I swivelled my attention slowly to Carnaby, who smiled weakly beneath pleading eyes. "Yes, quite, Wselfwulf sorted that all out quite handily. Tell me," I spoke to Cressida but continued observing Carnaby, "did Uncle

Wselfwulf also come to the rescue of my maiden aunt when she was accused of murder at Christmas?"

"You must be ever so grateful," contended Cressida.

"Eternally," I agreed. "It was a proper stumper, too." I leaned away from the table to allow the willowy Lint to remove my soup bowl. "Tell us, Wselfwulf, have you yet reached any conclusions regarding who might be behind Friday's tragic events?"

"We know who was *behind* it, Mister Busybeans..." Bunty didn't so much as struggle with my last name as dismiss it with a clip behind the ear. "...it was the curse."

"That's the general consensus then, is it?" I asked.

"We saw it, Anty." Cressida nodded at me with the same wide-eyed credulity that Carnaby had performed for me earlier.

"It's true, Anty." Barnaby spoke with an urbane indifference. "It's difficult for men of the world to countenance superstition, but one cannot dismiss the evidence of one's own eyes."

"There is no such thing," came a growing growl from the head of the table, "as the Carnaby Castle curse." Cecil Carnaby gavelled the table with his fist on the word 'curse'. "My wife was murdered, as likely as not by someone in this room."

I could have warned Cecil, as someone with greater than average familiarity with the phenomenon, that nothing dampens dinner chatter like accusations of murder, but he didn't ask. Hence silence reigned as Lint distributed the fish selection, which was an impossibly thin slice of local grayling through which I could see the pattern on the plate. Seasoned with lime and sea salt, however, and paired with a young but serviceable Chablis, it made for a very toothsome half-a-mouthful and primed me well for the main course.

Bunty toyed pettishly with her diaphanous serving of fish and mumbled something rebellious.

"What's that? Speak up, Bunty." Cecil pointed a menacing fish fork at his cousin. "If you have something to say then say it."

"You weren't even there," complied Bunty. "How can you say that the curse didn't fetch up Ludovica when you weren't even there?"

"For the same reason, Bunty, that I know my wife wasn't pushed to her death by leprechauns — because they don't exist. Are you really making the argument that I cannot deny the existence of something unless I've seen it?"

"Fair enough, Uncle," intervened Barnaby, "but that holds for your views as well — what possible reason could any of us have had to kill Ludovica?"

"Money, obviously. If I have children that'll just dilute the Carnaby fortune even further."

"What fortune?" laughed Cressida. "There's just a draughty castle. With a curse on it."

"Then why are you here?" countered Cecil. "Plenty of opportunities in London for hard-working young people. You ever meet any hard-working young people you should tell them that."

"Very droll, Uncle Cecil," said Barnaby. "We've as much right to be here as any Castle Carnaby."

"Sure, but, why?" asked Cecil.

"Eh?"

"Why?" repeated the patriarch with the tone of the belligerently baffled. "Why would you want to spend your youth haunting this mausoleum? Time I was your age, I'd helped push a railway through the Canadian wilderness. Shovelled coal on a merchant tramp to the Malay. I'd been shot — twice. I've forgotten more things I've done than you've actually done."

"I shall be returning to the capital shortly," answered Barnaby with cool pride. "I mean to continue reading for the law."

Cecil glowered at this specimen beneath hooded brows, which suddenly rose like springed shutters. "Reading for the law? Weren't you reading for the law last time I was here, what was it, five years ago?"

"Gentlemen feel no need to rush these things." Barnaby cast about the table for support and settled, doubtless by default, on me. "Isn't that so, Anty?"

"In the main, yes." The point was arguable, but I was replying in reflexive defence of the bullied. "Champers Monfoy — you know who I mean, Carnaby, president of the catering committee, can only drink cider before noon — has been reading for the bar for thirty-seven years. And that's not even a record for the Juniper. It's not even a record for the catering committee."

"There you go." Barnaby smiled triumphantly at Cecil.

"And what about you?" Cecil turned his attention, like an air-defence searchlight, on Cressida. "How are we going to marry you off if you're mooning about this pile of rocks all the time? Only bachelors dim and desperate enough are townies. You going to marry a towny?"

"Of course not," said Cressida with the wounded cry of the silver-spooned snob. She twirled a length of hair around a spindly index finger and gave me a side-long glance with the soft, seductive subtlety of a starter's pistol. "Who knows what favours the fates may bring to Hoy."

Even if it's me saying so, I'm rather a dab hand at the swift shift in subject. It is much commented upon at the club, where it often falls to me to act as conversational switch operator should Skewbald Runcorn get onto his favourite subject — why the government ought to abolish the peerage — or Sinjin Lord Ashby get onto his — why Skewbald Runcorn should shut his pie-hole. Typically a catalytic comment about the weather or veiled suggestion that I know something of value about the third race at Ally Pally will neatly avoid disaster. Rarely, though, do I have to use the talent in self-defence, but there I was, staring down the business end of a marriage-minded debutante, and I confess I wasn't in top form.

"Any theories why the curse elected to resume its interest in the castle?" I asked the assembly. I'm not saying it didn't work. It did. A perfect beamer, conversationally speaking, but it didn't so much divert conversation down another road as biff conversation in the back of the head with a paving stone.

Some weighty subtext descended on the table like damp canvas, and all was ominous silence.

Finally, Bunty murmured, "It was invited back." Rather cryptic, to my mind. The implication appeared to be that someone had sent the curse a friendly telegram suggesting that bygones should be bygones.

"It's castle property," insisted Cecil. "No reason that witch should have it rent-free."

"Forgive my homonyms, but to which witch do we refer?" I asked.

"The proprietress of the Castle Pub had been accustomed to paying rent on the property in kind," explained Carnaby.

"Kind?" barked Cecil. "Prancing about in her nightie under a full moon, pitching entrails at a chap? You call that payment in kind? I don't call that payment of any kind."

"It was her powers that protected the castle from the curse," Bunty mumbled at something beneath the table.

"Pah," opined Cecil.

"It can hardly be coincidence, Uncle," pointed out Cressida. "The very moment you come back and impose rent on Miss Kettle, the curse chucks your wife off the scarp."

Some instinct told me this witch angle would reward closer scrutiny, but in that moment, Prax wheeled a covered platter into the room. The intoxicating perfume of roast wild fowl reminded me that I'd given my last bun to Buns, and hadn't eaten since a late breakfast, if one doesn't count the equivalent of a shot glass of consommé and a transparent film of fish, and count them I did not.

Anticipation, as is so often the case, was followed by commensurate disappointment, as Prax snatched away the silver dome to reveal a pheasant the approximate size and weight of an adolescent parakeet. It was nicely dressed, however, and presented on a bed of roast potatoes beneath a blanket of woodberry glaze.

To compound the heartbreak, my share of the fledgling — a twiggy little wing that on its best day would have failed to give flight to the imagination — was sublime. Crisp and crackling and fresh with a thin glaze of bilberry and cranberry, it transported me, for about three seconds, to a walk in a winter wood. Presently, Lint cleared.

"If you don't believe in coincidence..." Cecil downed his cutlery as though to imbue the act with meaning, and pointed a resolute finger at Cressida. "...what do you call all your accidents?"

"Just that," said Cressida with a flick of insouciant hair, "accidents. It's an old castle, even by castle standards, and it's not as though we've been overzealous in keeping it up."

"What's this?" I asked. "Anything one should be particularly aware of if one is living, say, a hundred feet above ground in a thousand-year-old silo?"

"Just about everything," replied Barnaby. "Mainly falling through floors or being underneath other things that fall through floors. It is true, though, that for the last few weeks the old place has rather targeted Sid. You'd almost think that the castle or someone in it was trying to kill her."

CHAPTER SIX

The Many and Mounting Motives for Murder

"What ho, Castle-keep," I greeted Odd at, for me, the crack of dawn. Closer to nine-ish, actually, what with stopping for my ration of rasher at the castle, but I was otherwise shaken early from the sleep of the undernourished and drawn directly to the generous breakfast buffet of the Castle. "Pint of your finest cheddar, if you please."

Odd nodded me toward a sideboard, creaking with local produce and exotic artisanals from as far away as distant Derby, but I lingered at the opportunity to draw from the font of village lore that is the busy barkeep.

"I say, Odd old thing — odd old thing, there being two pubs in Hoy called 'The Castle', what?"

Odd regarded me beneath hooded brows as he hung tankards from hooks above the bar.

"There is no other pub in Hoy called the Castle, Mister Boisjoly." He spoke with a certain flat austerity, the way I've heard Ulster vicars contend that there's only one known version of *The Lord's Prayer.*

"Is this some sort of technicality?" I asked. "Is the other one actually, by some obscure zoning law, a butcher's?"

"There might be another pub in Hoy, but only one called the Castle."

"Right oh, then. This other pub, hypothetically speaking, would it be run by a woman of the singular name of Kettle?"

"Wandalen Kettle," confirmed Odd, but not without first glancing furtively about the empty barroom.

"I understand she has something of a sideline in the brisk curses and spells trade."

Odd steadied a fatherly eye on me. "Best to not talk of these things, Mister Boisjoly."

"Of course, what with the lingering threat of being turned into a frog."

"Worse than that."

"A Belgian?"

Odd placed his massive hands on the bar and leaned toward me, establishing a zone of confidence.

"Wandalen Kettle is in league with dark forces, Mister Boisjoly. You'd do well to stay clear of her."

"I appreciate your counsel very much, Odd," I said. "I'm going to ignore it, of course. In fact I am already doing so, but I want you to know that I value the spirit in which it is given. Nevertheless, you could reduce my exposure to the worry and bother of falling in love with a swan or being swindled out of the family cow for a bag of magic beans or what-have-you if you can just tell me this — does Miss Kettle pay rent on her nameless pub to the Castle Carnabys?"

"Some of the property on Carnaby Lane still belongs to the castle."

"Carnaby Lane — that would be the other street in Hoy, as compared to this one…"

"Carnaby Road."

"Of course. And Miss Kettle's establishment is one such address, I take it," I took it. "Is it also your understanding that the Kettle settles rental in services performed?"

Odd nodded with eyes closed, as though acknowledging the sinful state of man. "The Castle Carnabys are among the dark

49

forces to which I refer, Mister Boisjoly. Wandalen Kettle performs profane rites on their behalf."

"Word on the lane has it, Odd, that this arrangement has been brought to an end."

Odd gazed with dark surmise toward the door. "I wouldn't know — townies don't mix with Kettle or her kind — but it explains why the curse returned."

"So it is also your view, is it, Odd, that Miss Kettle stood sentry between the forces of evil and the town of Hoy?"

"Of course not," Odd scoffed.

"No, I find the notion a little flighty myself…"

"Wandalen Kettle stood between the forces of evil and the Castle Carnabys," clarified Odd. "She does nothing at all for the town of Hoy, except keep it under the heel of a line that should have died out a long time ago."

"Steady on."

"I don't wish harm on no-one in particular, you understand," said Odd in quick defence. "Just, the sooner there are no more Castle Carnabys, the sooner we're all Castle Carnabys, if you take my meaning."

"Candidly, Odd, I do not."

"The castle and a good part of the hill belong to the direct descendents of Ranulf Carnaby — the Castle Carnabys. When there aren't no more Castle Carnabys, the castle becomes community property."

"Morning, Boisjoly." Ivor's uncharacteristically spirited salutation took me sharp in the back of the neck, and when I turned he was flitting about the breakfast buffet like a butterfly, drunk with choice at Sissinghurst Flower Garden.

"What ho, 'spector," I said, reservedly, for over our long and largely pleasant acquaintance I've come to recognise the significance of certain humours exhibited by Ivor. "Have you made an arrest already?"

"Eh? No, no, not yet." Ivor levelled a thick layer of cold roast ham on his plate and then, on reflection, made it two. "I think the country air agrees with me. Have you seen this countryside? The mist settled in the valleys? I don't go in much for this poetry business, Boisjoly, but I swear this morning I caught myself lingering at my window, thinking, just, well, isn't that just something?"

"You know, I think that's a direct quote from Lord Byron's ode to Cyprus, 'Phoaw, Would You Look At That?' Doubtless you were similarly inspired."

I joined Ivor at the buffet and worked out a mainly cheddar-based strategy, not overlooking the ham, bacon, oatcakes, and fidgety pie. Ivor and I took the table by the fire and Odd perfected the picture with a piping pot of pekoe.

"How's life at the castle?" asked Ivor, after we'd both laid down a safe, base foundation.

"Spartan," I replied. "Do you know the secret to feeding six hungry adults with a single runt quail?"

"I wouldn't have thought you could."

"That is, in fact, the secret." I held a morsel up to the light and mused wistfully on the poetry that is English hard cheese. "The silver lining is that dinner served as little distraction from the affectionate repartée of the Carnaby Parliament."

"Learn anything valuable?"

"More a surface sense, really, of mutual and profound acrimony," I replied. "However I have assembled a large portfolio of motives through which you may wish to browse, with a little something for everyone."

"Such as?" Ivor said this as a prelude to ingesting a strip of ham ingeniously rolled around a dab of mustard. He appeared distracted, if not entirely detached.

"Well, let's see, what's your fancy? We have several variations on the oldest motive of all, of course."

"Jealousy?"

"Second oldest then — money. Cecil Carnaby believes that his wife was murdered by a fellow Castle Carnaby to prevent her and, more particularly, her offspring, from diluting the family fortune."

"Yes," said Ivor, pausing for liquid intake. "He advanced that theory rather forcefully when Blewit and I interviewed him."

"Where is our boy in blue today, by the way?"

"Chesterfield, making enquiries."

"At the telegraph office," I surmised. "I think you'll find that it was the butler, Wurt, who sent the cable to Carnaby two weeks ago, and I think you'll further find that the butler, Wurt, has no recollection of the event. But I carry on presuming that Blewit is wiring London for a little biographical background on the man calling himself Elwin Smith."

Ivor nodded. "Curious chap. Clearly a false name, but he can back it up with an eclectic array of documentation. He's got a Caterpillar Club pin — you won't believe the membership requirements."

"You have to have parachuted to safety from a doomed aircraft."

"That's right." Ivor paused a consignment of bacon. "How the devil..."

"Enoch Cardall — we call him Euchre at the club, obviously — lobbied for membership," I explained. "They're quite strict about their entry criteria, though, and it turns out the aeroplane has to have actually left the ground. Did Elwin — in the questionable habit of calling himself Win, by the way — offer any proof of identity that couldn't be easily forged?"

Ivor sipped his tea noncommittally. "That's not a very broad field... French driving permit, endorsed for going sixty miles an hour in a quarry... letter disinviting him to join the Shackleton–Rowett Expedition to the South Pole."

"Conspicuous by its absence is anything issued by his majesty's government. Practically a confession. Still, doesn't make him a murderer."

"We know he's not," said Ivor. "He was nowhere near the other side of the hill when Mrs Carnaby was, in the words of practically everyone, 'fetched up'."

"Where was he?"

"Cemetery, of all places. He says that he was looking for ancestors. He saw and was seen by Cecil Carnaby, who was occupied with a similar undertaking."

"Neatly ruling out the grieving husband, too, I note," I said. "Might they know one another? They strike me as cast from the same tramp-steaming, quarry-defacing mould."

"Possibly, but they were both seen by the proprietress of the other Castle Pub."

"Wandalen Kettle," I added.

"Correct. And if she's harbouring any affection for Cecil Carnaby she hides it with steely resolve."

"Which brings us to the next item in our catalogue," I said. "Apparently among his first official acts as castle despot, Cecil cancelled a long-standing arrangement with Miss Kettle, the terms of which included free use of the pub premises in exchange for professionally performed poppycock; the Kettle is — or was — the Carnaby house witch."

"So the motive is revenge?" speculated Ivor.

"Fear," I corrected. "There are those — a disturbingly large number of those, in point of fact — who can't see the cobblers for the curse. Obviously Miss Kettle withdrew her services and that may have led one or more of the Castle Carnabys to fear for their lives, and lay the blame at the ample feet of Cecil."

"Just the female Castle Carnabys, though," pointed out Ivor.

"And those that love them," I said. "So, yes, just the women. The curse is apparently quite specific about that."

"All about preventing resident Carnabys from extending the line, I understand."

"Which reminds me, Inspector, of a late addition to the lineup — a lovely bit of avarice, well-used but good as new — it turns out that if and when the Castle Carnaby line reaches the terminus the castle and its remaining holdings become the property of the town."

"I know," said Ivor, knowingly. "Stands to reason, doesn't it? Town Carnabys are still Carnabys, but so far removed from the original family line that no one of them could ever prove primogeniture. The estate would be divided evenly."

"And this occurs now, assuming he doesn't find an understudy for the role of Ludovica Carnaby, with the passing of Cecil," I surmised.

"Apparently not. Until there are no more direct male descendants, Ranulf Carnaby's original will applies, legally speaking — Castle Carnabys have right of residence. Cecil Carnaby can't sell anything or deny his cousins the pleasure of the castle, but eldest resident male has executive power."

"So, Cecil only *acts* like he owns the joint. He's very anxious to see Nobby and Sid find happiness in London or, at the very least, somewhere else."

"Nobby and Sid?"

"Barnaby and Cressida Carnaby, niece and nephew to the philosopher king," I explained. "Hard to say what their motive might be, apart from thinning the herd. Or possibly preserving the legacy for their respective eventual offspring."

"Neither of them are even married," noted Ivor.

"Not as of latest dispatch," I confirmed. "But I'm very careful to not let Sid get anywhere near my ring finger — she strikes me as a girl with a mission. Possibly a race against the fates — did she mention that the castle itself appears to have taken a personal interest in her welfare?"

"In passing." Ivor finished his breakfast with a *coup de grace* of cheddar, ham, crunchy crust, and bacon, and leaned away from the table with his teacup like a man with a yearning to loosen his belt. "She mentioned a number of accidents. Anything in it, you think?"

"The incidents appear innocent enough, taken on their own," I said. "An apparently notoriously cantankerous lock on the wine cellar trapped her inside when the family thought that she'd gone to Chesterfield to be fitted for something — a sequined wedding dress, no doubt — she'd have been undiscovered for days had Wurt not developed a sudden thirst to take inventory."

"Sort of thing that probably happens all the time in a pile that age."

"Just so," I agreed. "As is the case with the rampart which, after a thousand years of loyal service, fell on the time and place where Sid likes to go for a restorative gasper after meals — missed her by an ash, to hear her and Nobby tell it."

"Again, it's an old place."

"Well that's just it, isn't it?" I said. "A millennium of peaceful coexistence with the clan Carnaby, and only two weeks ago the castle picks its target, starting with a creosote explosion in Sid's chimney that might easily have killed her had she not been protected by a layer of sequins."

"Could be coincidence."

"Could be," I granted. "Could be the Carnaby Castle Curse, too, or a targeted campaign of harassment by Carpenter ants, but I doubt it. So does Sid, to hear her dismiss it. As it stands, Bunty — that's Mrs Stokely — seems to fear the curse the most."

"So I observed when we interviewed her," recalled Ivor. "But I note that she also fears storms, strangers, uniformed police officers, being alone, and having too many people about. In any case, isn't the curse primarily concerned with preventing the continuation of the Castle Carnaby line? I can't imagine Mrs Stokely — a widow, incidentally — is a likely vessel to carry the lineage into the future."

"Deftly put, Inspector. Maybe the curse knows something we don't. I was thinking of having a look for myself at Hoy Scarp this afternoon, after which I mean to make a study of the living parable that is the household staff — the drunk, the gifted, and the linty."

"Be my guest. We've had our crack at them. Closed-mouthed brigade, for the most part."

"This is because you present a towering figure of authority, Inspector." I raised my teacup in salute to his towering authority. "You have bearing. Gravitas. That moustache. Whereas I'm received merely as a friend of the family and, thanks to Carnaby, not even a particularly clever one."

Ivor raised a curious eyebrow.

"Carnaby has been living vicariously through what I hope it's not a stretch to call 'our' adventures," I explained. "In retelling them at the castle, he's cast himself in the role of handsome young amateur sleuth with a quick wit, happy disposition, and the universal admiration of Scotland Yard."

"Bit of a liberty."

"Big as the statue thereof," I agreed. "But, frankly, I'm not half flattered. And it's gratifying to know that Carnaby has such depth — had you asked me yesterday I'd have said his greatest ambition was to be regarded as the kingdom's foremost expert on decanting. In any case, it allows me to move freely about the castle, disguised as the half-witted houseguest. I've been practising vacant stares in the mirror."

"Yes, quite convincing."

"I'm not doing one now," I corrected. "That's just the Boisjoly eyebrows working their magic. Now, I hope I've been of some service in complicating the investigation, Inspector." I drained my teacup and plucked up my hat. "Shall we reconvene the committee here this evening, say... feast o'clock?"

"Haven't you overlooked a Castle Carnaby on your list of suspects?"

"You mean Barnaby Carnaby?" I asked. "He shows limited promise, I fear. His sole aspiration appears to mirror almost perfectly that of Carnaby the club steward — he wants to be me, just more debonnaire, the poor nit."

"It's to your club steward that I refer."

"Old Wselfwulf?" I scoffed. "I've told you, the man is as correct as an imperial ounce. He would never resort to violence, except in the name of king and country and, probably, decorum. In any case, he had no motive."

"Well, there's power. That's very often a motive."

"Power? What sort of power?"

"Over the castle and its properties," said Ivor. "Should the death of Ludovica Carnaby drive Cecil back into exile, as seems very probable, Wselfwulf Carnaby would resume his role as family patriarch."

CHAPTER SEVEN

The Unstoppable Start for the Top of the Scarp

The river was casting off its blanket of morning fog and bubbling up to another busy day of spinning mill wheels and bouncing punts against each other beneath the stone bridge next to the cemetery.

I stood on the bridge and admired the hard-working stream cascading toward me from the other side of the hill, wishing I had its strength of character. Owing to what I regard as a wholly rational wariness of high places, I had elected to begin my examination of the scarp from the bottom, and in that moment realised that this meant a considerable hike upriver.

"You are a friend of the crow."

This contention came to me on the wind, as of fog made audible and showing early signs of Smoker's Lung. A weedy, wispy figure stood in the mist at the door of the catacomb, all alabaster skin and obsidian hair, loosely layered in ribbon and wraps of black leather, linen and lace — exactly how I imagined Buns would look if he were trying to impersonate Lucrezia Borgia. She made for a striking figure, particularly in light of my impression that she hadn't been there a second ago.

"Anthony Boisjoly," I said. "Anty to crows and all fellow friends thereof. Miss Wandalen Kettle, I believe."

Wandalen awarded me the point with a grave nod of the head.

"You are a seeker of truth, Anty."

"I am," I confirmed. "Got any?"

"You wish to know about the curse."

"Only peripherally," I said. "For instance, why do so many people in this town believe in fairy tales in this, the age of powered flight and the electric chafing dish?"

"The curse has been part of the fabric of Hoy for four hundred years," said Wandalen, as though it explained something.

"Has it?" I asked. "I understood that it was on something of a sabbatical until recently."

Wandalen inclined her head in that slow, sage nod of the theatrically inscrutable. "Until last week, when I was forced to withdraw my protection, the curse had claimed no one for thirty-five years."

"You're not going to tell me that you've been minding the vexes for thirty-five years," I said. "You must have been a very gifted newborn. One of those protégés, were you?"

"I inherited my powers — and the Castle Pub — from my mother."

"That makes marginally more sense, I suppose."

"Do you not believe in curses, Anty?"

"I've often suspected that sometime in, I would say, my nineteenth year, I irked a gipsy at the racetrack," I confessed. "But in principle, no, not a lot. Nice living, is it? Much overhead? Easy workload?"

The witch shrugged. "Mainly spells, incantations, rituals, little light conjuring around first harvest."

"Until Cecil Carnaby ended the arrangement."

"Wselfwulf and I had a loose understanding, and at any rate he was always in London," reminisced Wandalen. "Then Cecil came back from bouncing about the world, all full of cynical, modern ideas, and he took over the running of the castle. First day back he came into the pub to collect the rent."

"And he wouldn't listen to what passes for reason in Hoy?"

"He was quite dismissive about my vocation." Wandalen raised an aggrieved chin. "I warned him what was at stake, you know. I told him the same thing that happened to Capricia Carnaby would happen to his Ludovica."

"What did happen to her?"

"Like I say — same thing that happened to Ludovica. She was fetched up by the mists."

"Thirty-five years ago." I performed some light mental maths. "She wasn't also Cecil's bride, was she?"

"No, of course not," scoffed Wandalen. "He wasn't even here, in those days. He's only a Castle Carnaby by birth. No, Capricia Carnaby was engaged to be married to Loftis Carnaby, a distant cousin."

"Wasn't that just baiting the curse?"

"Capricia was blinded by love, as young girls so often are," said Wandalen. "Indeed, according to my mother, Loftis was a physically repellent man, with a soap allergy that was the subject of much comment as far away as Chesterfield."

"Didn't the family try to stop her?" I asked.

"The family welcomed the union. I believe the attitude toward the curse among Castle Carnabys, at the time, was much like your own. They soon learned to respect the power of witchcraft." Wandalen fixed me with the cold, portentous eye of a cocktail hour *maitre d'hotel*. "As will you."

"If you're about to foretell the dire fate that will befall me after I've become king of the Scots, I don't want to hear it." I held up my stifling hand. "I want it to be a surprise."

"It was to be the day of the wedding," continued Wandalen. "And though it was clear and bright, as the bride walked the scarp, a mist came spilling over the edge. She looked back to the wedding party, rejoicing on the lawn, and as they all watched, she was snatched away."

"Something uncannily similar happened to a fellow Juniper, Tuck Tilbury, on his wedding day at Saint Botolph Without Aldgate, although his bride didn't so much 'disappear' as 'board a ship bound for America with her dressage coach', but the effect is largely the same — warm champagne, and plenty of it."

"This is quite different."

"That's true, in many respects," I conceded. "For instance, my story is fact-based. Talking of which, I understand that you were here when the mists gathered up Cecil Carnaby's bride."

"Who told you that?"

"Inspector Wittersham. We tell each other everything. Gets positively embarrassing sometimes."

"I was at the Castle," countered Wandalen.

"The pub, you mean." I nodded to the pub in question, across the graveyard, opposite the entrance. "I understand that you were nevertheless able to give Cecil Carnaby an alibi."

Wandalen nodded. "I saw him from the window. Ten minutes later he came into the pub with Elwin Smith."

"You're quite sure of the time."

Wandalen nodded in a north-easterly direction. "T'was as the life-giving orb withdrew beyond the edge of knowing."

"Sunset, you mean."

"In a word. Maybe a few minutes later. The inspector tells me that's the moment when Ludovica Carnaby was fetched up."

"I'll bet he didn't use those words," I safely ventured. "Thank you, Miss Wandalen, for your cryptic concern for my welfare. You'll be pleased to know that I'll be examining the scene of the crime from the safety of the river bed."

"You fear heights."

"Irrational, I know," I confessed. "I have a wholly illogical phobia of mad dogs and dark alleys, too. Consequences of a shielded upbringing, I expect."

Wandalen reached into the recesses of her silk substratum and withdrew a little glass vial, sealed with a tiny cork and hanging from a thin chain. Inside was what looked like live mould, or a bit of tar.

"Take this unguent. Hold it beneath your tongue before bearding that which unnerves you. It will allow you to face your fears."

"No thanks," I demurred. "It wouldn't do to be much braver. It would only make me foolhardy. Well, to be pedantic, *more* foolhardy."

"It's also good for nightmares."

"Still…"

"And hangovers."

"I'll take two."

The valley formed between Hoy and two neighbouring hills to the west and north rose in a gently exhausting manner as it curved out of sight. The river took on a consequently more business-like attitude and largely ignored me as I picked my way along the little tow-path. It took me about twenty-five minutes to hike from the cemetery to the place described by Ivor as that where Ludovica Carnaby met her rocky end. He wouldn't have needed to.

The point of impact was marked by a nasty bullseye of a round rock, smoothed by the centuries but clearly solid enough for the dark work to which it had been put. I followed the obvious trajectory up a chunky, lumpy, sandstone cliff-face rising a hundred feet above, topped with an overhanging mop of moss. As I looked up, a cloud passed overhead and beyond the top of the cliff, and in that conspiracy common to clouds and tall buildings it created the brief but vivid illusion that the entire hill was falling over. I felt compelled to sit on one of the piles of a little pier, and watch the water for a tick or two.

I audited close horizontal space for a bit. It was a nice spot, in closeup — bouncily uneven and formed of river-rounded rocks, porous pours of tempered lava, pebbles and spikey gritstone shards that had long ago slid down the cliffside. It was quiet, apart from the river, and isolated at a point where the valley curved around Hoy Hill, roughly crosswise from the town. I noted that, possibly owing to that feature, a little cove around a flat rock showed evidence of having been employed for some ritual — there were crimson stains on the surface and a pattern of small bones had been scattered on the ground. It was evidently a popular venue for composition of the spirit and fabrication of courage, and that's what I did.

Thusly becalmed, I allowed myself to muse on some manner in which a gifted climber might make his way from the riverbed to the top of the scarp and, presumably, back down again. I'm far from an expert — more in the way of a keen non-participant — but a possible ascent came to me in a set of stairs, formed of carved rock, planks, and rope bannisters, and weaving a zig-zag pattern up the cliff-side.

The thing about climbing a cliff, even via the relative safety of stairs formed of slippy stone and wet-weakened wood, is there's no halfway point. I mean to say, there's no clear delineation between, 'well, that's high enough, guess I'll safely descend' and 'it's far too late to safely descend.' All of a sudden, there I was.

I put my back to the wall of cold rock and braced myself against winds that had a wholly opposing agenda. Snatching a furtive glance at the rocky shore some two miles below me, I recalled the little vial of placebo that Wandalen had sold me for what seemed now a quite economical four shillings six. I reached it from my pocket and, as an added precaution, closed my eyes.

As I placed a half a prescription beneath my tongue I strongly suspected that the Hoy village witch had sold me a quarter ounce of processed liquorice root — which I loathe — for four shillings six, but the whipping wind and another ill-advised glance toward the ground — which had by then dropped to a distance of at least five miles — gave me a renewed will to believe almost anything.

Newly brave, I hung the vial from my neck and climbed exactly one more step before the wind, twisted and amplified by the valley, took a new tack and started throwing things. A tangled black mass slapped against the rock face in an explosion of feathers and fluttered to the steps. Dazed, Buns staggered in a circle and then looked up at me with an incredulous shake of the head.

"Poor weather for aviation, Buns old man," I shouted over the wind. "I propose that we achieve the summit on foot."

The bird hopped cautiously ahead, step by step, and alternated paternal glances back to verify that I had yet to fall to my death. It was heartening, and I daresay either Wandalen's unguent worked or I responded well to mutual mortal panic.

"Steady on, Buns," I laughed with the high-spirited fatalism I like to imagine characterised the banter of the Last March of the Terra Nova expedition to the South Pole. "You're not going to let a little wind and a little dizzying altitude dampen your alpine spirit — I've got a bun in my pocket that says you won't."

Buns hurried on ahead while I maintained a sure, steady pace of roughly one step per hundred beats of a coward's heart. Presently the tuft of moss came into view and I crawled onto it like a child and then rolled down a short incline to safety and shelter from the wind.

"Cor," commented Buns, with wonder in his voice.

"The *mot juste*," I agreed, and I handed over the promised breakfast roll. "Today I have renewed an already lively appreciation for flat surfaces, Buns old thing. I'm glad you were here to share the moment."

A wooden barrier between me and the abyss gave me confidence to stand and take in the expansive view. From the top of the scarp the northern majesty of the White Peak spread out in a tapestry of hills and gorges, rivers and forests, clouds on the peaks and mists in the valleys. It was clear how those gazing on this shifting, living masterpiece four hundred years ago might have believed in magic. Frankly, in that moment, it was difficult not to.

This was the spot from which Ravena Sooter, speaking her last words, made them count. Then she was pitched over the edge and into the very heart of Carnaby family mythology. In the instant, she probably regretted that she wasn't really a witch and, in equal measure, claiming that she was.

In the direction of safety, the expanse from Hoy Scarp to the back of Carnaby Castle was largely unkept scrubland, the broad, black skeletons of a few expired elms, a clothesline, and a neat little garden at what I assume was the kitchen door. The castle extended from one side of the plateau to the other and no one could have crossed from it to the scarp without being seen by anyone even casually observing the lawn.

The neat little garden was tended by a neat little Prax Carnaby. I spotted the prim cook as she pulled a brace of turnips from the earth with a proud delight, as though the little bulbs had exceeded all the secret hopes she'd dared place in them.

"Lovely morning," I asserted, by way of warning of incoming Boisolys.

"Hullo," said Prax with an implied 'what's all this then?' "It's Mister Boisjoly, isn't it? Where have you come from?"

"River," I said with a casual gesture of the head. "I was examining the coastline."

"You came up over the side," observed Prax.

"Oh, did I?" I looked back at Hoy Scarp. "Yes, quite right, I believe I did. Just out for a wander, you see, and that cliff somehow got in the way. One barely notices these things."

"You have moss in your hair."

"Has that yet to catch on up here in Derbyshire?" I asked. "Prax Carnaby, isn't it? I very much enjoyed my morsel of pheasant last night. The woodberry sauce could have stood on its own, as indeed it very nearly did."

Prax smiled modestly but sincerely. "You'll never guess my secret ingredient..."

"Gin."

"How the devil? There was barely a drop."

"It's a gift," I said. "Couldn't tell you the distillery, though. Plymouth, obviously, but beyond that I'm baffled. You didn't hone this exceptional talent here at Castle Carnaby."

"Not entirely, no." Prax shook the excess dirt off her turnips with indulgent admonishment, as a kindly nanny might relieve a child of something he's found in a puddle. "I've been lucky enough to make my way on my meagre talents. I worked on the continent — the *Riviera Royale* and *Les Deux Moulins* — and in America, for a bit. I was sous-chef in the upper day kitchen on the *Prinses Grietje* when it used to tour the orient."

"Done any chuckwagonning?"

"Five-day cattle drive, Texas to Nevada, in 1918. It's when I learned to make corn dodgers."

"That's handy, I suppose, in the event of heavy cornfall," I said. "Where did you learn to combine gin and wildfowl?"

"That's my own invention." Prax smiled coyly. "Although it was inspired by my time as cook at Doby Hall. Do you know Lord Llannybidder?"

"That explains it," I said. "The man puts gin in practically everything. It's all right when you know to expect it, but you'll want to be on your guard if he ever offers you a cup of tea. Carries a flask of the stuff about him at all times as though it were, say, an unguent against evil forces."

"Speaking of such," Prax gestured with her turnips toward the little jar of lies hanging around my neck. "I had the impression you didn't believe in that sort of thing."

"A gift," I said, looking down at it. "I say gift — four shillings six, and it tastes like ear medicine. I take it you do believe in that sort of thing."

"I saw what happened with my own eyes, Mister Boisjoly — Ludovica Carnaby was taken up by the mists and pulled right over the side of the scarp."

"You don't think it's more likely she was pushed — or pulled — by human hand?"

"Not from where I was standing."

"Which was where, roughly?"

"There, exactly." Prax pointed with her nose either at or over my left shoulder. "North tower."

We both took in the awesome structure. Like the south tower I called home, the entrance to the north tower was at the allure and the first window that wasn't accidental was about forty feet above ground.

"I understand that this was sometime in the early evening."

"Sunset, on the button." Prax regarded the western horizon with a curious surmise, as though just then noticing the peculiar coincidence of the sun so often setting there. "The long shadows stopped at the very moment that Ludovica went over the side."

"And you can think of no one in the castle who might wish to do her harm."

"No..." Prax mused on the notion. "Apart from just about everyone, I mean. They all hated her."

"Surely not Cecil."

"No, I mean every other Castle Carnaby."

"Surely not Wselfwulf."

"Particularly Mister Wselfwulf. He's the one who levelled the charge before she even got here."

"Charge?" I asked. "What charge?"

"They all thought that Ludovica Carnaby was after their money."

CHAPTER EIGHT

The Legion
Layers of Lint

I made my farewells to Prax and her turnips, both of which I looked forward to seeing later, when I spotted Lint the maid through a steamy window.

The kitchen had the worn, prehistoric quality of your finer castle sculleries — smooth and uniform with age, such that everything appeared carved into a single block of granite. Iron pots and pans and wooden utensils hung from the ceiling over a stone and metal cooking surface. Against the opposite wall was a still life of potatoes and turnips on a nicked and battered oaken table. The air was a thick, immobile haze.

As I entered the kitchen, my senses were tested by a dense vapour, apparently spilling over the edges of a cauldron that Lint was agitating with an oar on a hot iron stove.

"Whatever that is," I opined, "It's already got far too much gin in it."

Lint, finely turned out in a wrinkled pinafore that looked like the field of a recent battle of attrition between all the socks in the house, turned to me without missing a stroke. "It's Mister Wurt's morning suit, sir."

"Oh, right, well, I stand corrected. Probably just the right amount. Lindingfleis, isn't it?"

"Call me Lint, sir."

"I'll do my best. Can't promise consistency, though," I said. "The cheeky *surnom* is all very good when it's a fellow clubman

— almost a house rule, in fact — but nicknames typically aren't so... ehm..."

"Accurate, sir?"

"For want of a more diplomatic word, yes," I agreed. "There are rare exceptions, of course — Vats Swillingdon, for instance, and Spins Purley. Spins once became nauseous watching me turn up a piano stool. But this is the market in manners of men on equal social standing. Perhaps not Vats — he's in the Privy Council."

"I don't mind, sir," said Lint with resolute cheer. "I know what I look like, and I like how I look. It's what you might call a statement."

"A sort of protest, manifest in fibre and floss."

"If you like, yes."

"And what are you protesting?"

"My station, I suppose, if I have to put a word to it."

"You don't absolutely have to," I allowed. "But it will keep conversation ticking over. You don't care for serving at table and boiling the fumes out of morning suits?"

"I don't mind the work." Lint emphasised the point with a good churn of the suit-pot. "I like to be useful. That's just the problem though, isn't it? There's nothing useful about doing for a family of idle swellings. They get all the Lindingfleis they deserve, and that's just Lint."

"They do keep you employed."

"Begging your pardon, sir," corrected Lint. "They keep me down, is what they do. If the Castle Carnabys would just hurry up and die out then something could be made of this place. An hotel, maybe, or a spa. Miss Prax could be a chef again, and I'd be head of household. Mister Wurt... well..."

"I suggest Master of Revels, if it's not overstepping my capacity as confidante. The man is a juggernaut."

"Something would be found for Mister Wurt." Lint returned to her sculling with a therapeutic hostility. "No point in thinking about all that, though. Not while there are Castle Carnabys."

"That's a rapidly developing state of affairs, what with the rate at which Castle Carnabys are dropping off scarps," I observed. "By my calculations, that's one a week since Monday last. At this rate they'll be entirely wiped out by Spring Bank Holiday."

"You're a curious sort, aren't you sir?" Lint ceased her stirrings and put up her oar.

"In what sense?" I asked. "I mean to say, yes, and proudly so, however you mean it, but one likes to be concise. For instance, I'm curious to know what you saw last Friday evening."

Lint hooked the morning suit out of the cauldron, like a great, damp effigy of a drowned butler.

"Same as you was told last night at dinner." Lint boldly and casually kicked over the pretension that staff are deaf to what the quality say at mealtimes. "Mrs Ludovica was fetched up by the mists."

"And where were you?"

"Standing right where I am now." Which was, now that she'd pulled the heap of wool away from the stove, directly in front of the window.

"And what were you doing, if you recall."

"Same thing I am now." Lint didn't actually follow this up with a long, resigned, existential sigh, but it was strongly implied. "Boiling sheets."

"And you clearly saw what happened," I said. "Through that window."

The panes of the window in question were now almost entirely opaque with steam.

"I saw well enough," maintained Lint. "And it's what everybody saw, wasn't it?"

"With almost uncanny consistency, yes. It was early evening, though, and the window was quite steamy. Wouldn't the reflecting sunset have interfered with visibility?"

"There was no sun by the time it happened," said Lint, dubiously, as though unsure of or just realising the detail. "In fact, it dropped away at the same instant as Mrs Ludovica did."

"How cinematic. What happened then?"

"I went for help."

"Did you find any?"

"Not really. There was Mister Wurt, and Mrs Stokely. They were in the courtyard, but Mrs Stokely was beside herself with fright, and Wurt was... well, Wurt was how he always is by sunset."

"You didn't see Wselfwulf? Or Prax?"

"Prax, yes. She came from the guard house some five minutes later. She told us that Cecil was in the graveyard, and she sent Wurt to fetch him."

A sudden, scandalised, vaguely accusatory "Lint!" came to us from the door, and Bunty Stokely made a dramatic entrance.

"Mister Boisjoly, please leave us," she said. "I would have words with my maid."

"Right ho," I said, and started for the door.

"One moment, Mister Boisjoly. Please remain. I wish to have a witness on hand."

"Right ho right ho," I agreed. "Saves me the indignity of eavesdropping."

"Lint, my amulet is missing from my room."

"What's that to do with me?" inquired Lint, flatly, with no hint of offence or, really, interest.

"You're the only one with a key," prosecuted Bunty. "And the room was locked."

"You've probably misplaced it, Mrs Stokely," said Lint with patient indifference. "Where have you looked?"

"Lost it? I would never lose it. It's probably the only thing keeping me alive. You must return it at once."

"I never touched your horrid amulet," protested Lint. "Let's go have a look."

The castle kitchen is built into the back wall, and so if you want to get to the north tower you've got the choice of either changing your mind or walking through the courtyard. We went with the latter option and soon we were winding up a dark, dangerous, dingy set of stairs that rang with sentimental inklings of my own tower of death. Both towers had unusually thick walls that, pared back a bit, could have accommodated a very welcome lift. Each had a door to the allure that was bolted from the inside and hence was only accessible, without explicit invitation, from the door in the courtyard.

Bunty's room, too, was like mine in that it was on what would be the second floor if mediaeval towers had floors, as such, and her balcony looked north while mine looked south. It was far more selectively decorated than my room and hence much cosier, cluttered with overstuffed floor pillows and a bulging divan and four-poster bed the mattress of which looked like it had enjoyed an idle life of unrestrained gluttony. Above the fireplace, which was neatly maintained and secured with a locked grate, was some sort of pagan symbol knotted out of baler twine.

Bunty pointed with scandalised awe at the open French doors to the balcony, between which stood a plaster bust of Athena on a nightstand.

"It was right there, in the window, gaining power from the sun." Bunty squinted conspiratorially at me. "And now it's gone."

"And you're quite sure that the door was locked?" I asked.

"I never leave my room unlocked," she insisted. "I don't even usually leave my room, and certainly not without my amulet. Now that Wandalen Kettle no longer protects us it's the only thing standing between me and the curse." Her face softened with an ill-fitting deliberate diplomacy that she turned on Lint. "Please, Lint, I'll pay you to return it."

"I don't have your ugly amulet, Mrs Stokely." Lint's cool composure in the face of parliamentary-grade libel suggested that she had form fielding such accusations.

"Why don't you borrow Miss Cressida's amulet — she never wears it."

"But if you didn't take it, who did?" Bunty cast an apprehensive squint over the Boisjoly profile, like a hen who's just begun to suspect this strangely charming fox might be up to no good.

I, in the meantime, was examining the bust of Athena, who presented as notably demure, considering her reputation. Taking the perspective of the goddess of war, wisdom, and wittling, I could clearly see the scarp, but only the scarp. At that height and a safe distance from the edge, the rest of the garden was almost entirely obscured by balcony.

"I understand that this is where you were on Friday night, when the curse claimed Ludovica."

A shadow that Poe would probably have described as 'spectral' fell over Bunty's face, and her eyes widened in what I had come to regard as a quaint castle custom.

"She was taken up by the mists."

"This is an excellent vista, I would think, for curse-watching," I observed. "See anything else, by chance? Or anyone?"

"There was only Ludovica," marvelled Bunty. "And the mists."

"And twilight. A most complete confluence of mystic weather conditions."

"No, the sun had yet to set," recollected Bunty.

"Had yet to set?" I asked. "Are you quite sure?"

"Of course I'm sure."

"How obsequious sunset is in the Peak District," I opined. "It's all things to all people."

"It's the altitude, isn't it," said Lint. "We're fifty feet above ground, so sunset takes a bit longer."

"Of course." I dared lean out over the balcony and steal a glance at the decidedly distant ground. "And it must be another hundred feet again above the cemetery."

"Probably more," said Lint.

"Is this helping find my amulet?" asked Bunty from heretofore hidden depths of snark.

"Indirectly," I assured her. "I find the discussion of the physical properties of light and hilltops intellectually stimulating, and that's got to push things along. When did you last see it?"

"An hour ago. I only left it for a few minutes. I needed a book from the library, but the sun was just right..." Bunty looked longingly at the naked neck of Athena. "...and I could tell that it was losing power. When I came back it was gone."

"That settles that, then," concluded Lint. "I've been in the kitchen the whole morning. You can ask Miss Prax or Mister Boisjoly here."

"You could do," I confirmed. "But you'd just hear the same tired story. You say the amulet draws its power from the sun."

"Or the moon." Bunty nodded firmly. "They're mystical, you see. Wandalen and her mother have always made gifts of the amulets to the Castle Carnaby women."

"When you say gift..."

"There is, by convention, a small honorarium."

"I'll just bet there is," I said.

"It's only just," insisted Bunty. "The amulets prevent the curse from taking us... Cressida! I must have Cressida's amulet."

Bunty rushed from the room, stopped at the top of the stairs, and then descended them slowly and methodically. Lint turned a 'see what I have to deal with?' expression on me.

"Think this lot deserves more than Lint?"

"Let's follow, and find out," I proposed.

Lint locked Bunty's room for her and we tracked the dowager at a safe distance. She paused at the door to the courtyard and surveyed the terrain for, presumably, mists or their emissaries. Then she scampered across the courtyard like a skittish doe in bedroom slippers and disappeared through the door of the castle keep.

"They'll be in the library," said Lint, and returned to her thankless and, almost certainly, fruitless task of boiling Wurt's morning suit.

The library in the castle keep was on the top floor and unlike most other rooms in the castle in that it was larger — it appeared to have been the result of the walls between several drab cells knocked through to make one grand, drab cell, with books and a harpsichord. The books were the weighty, unreadable volumes that the authorities in such things issue to the private libraries of great houses, manors, and castles, and the harpsichord was in current use as a games table and drinks trolley. The three walls without books were hung with thick tapestries and the furniture which wasn't a harpsichord was a low table, on which lay a tea set, and a chaise longue, on which lay a Cressida. I arrived at the door the moment Bunty discovered the scene.

"Cressida, dear," said Bunty with a false bonhomie that rather let the 'false' part do most of the heavy lifting.

Cressida replied without looking up from a March, 1927 edition of *Pall Mall*. "Yes, Bunty?"

"Cressida, I must have your amulet."

"What's wrong with yours? Is it lonely?"

"Lint has pinched it."

"I don't think that's been conclusively proven," I pointed out from the door.

"Thank you, Mister Boisjoly," said Bunty flatly. "But that is hardly the point. Please, Cressida. May I have it?"

"I don't have it anymore." Cressida looked up, briefly, and then returned her attention to her magazine. "Mine's been stolen too."

"That's an intriguing coincidence," I said. "When did this happen?"

"This morning sometime." Cressida turned an impartial page. "Must have happened during breakfast."

"Was your room locked?" asked Bunty in an awed whisper.

"I suppose it was, now you mention it."

"You're quite sure?" I asked.

"Oh, very," assured Cressida. "If I don't lock my room Nobby nicks my cigarettes."

"Does anyone else have a key?"

"The maid, I think. But she served at breakfast."

"Leaving us with, in addition to an impossible murder," I chorused in the Greek tradition, "two locked room mysteries."

"I suppose so," agreed Cressida in the lowest of keys. "I wonder how the thief did it?"

"More worrying, Cressida, is why." Bunty furrowed her brow and kneaded her hands and sat at the harpsichord. "Who would want to leave us unprotected against the curse?"

CHAPTER NINE

It All Began at Christmas in Milan

I've stayed at countless great houses and castles and the like over the years and, among rather a lot of other cultural and concrete characteristics, they all share a certain routine. It's that calendar and catalogue of convention formed of social norms and whatever eccentricities the place has evolved for itself. Handsome Hall, for instance, the country seat of Lord Stibling, Master of the Horse and distant Boisjoly kin, still announces dinner with the firing of a cannon from the north battlements. Not a small cannon, either, and it's just not the sort of thing you can be warned against, particularly if your first time hearing it you're standing up in a skiff on the duck pond.

Carnaby Castle was not like that. As mentioned, there wasn't even a dinner gong and tea, so far as I could discern, was pursued in the independent, swashbuckling spirit of 'devil take the hindmost.' This suited my purposes, partially because it freed me to convene a committee of concern with Inspector Wittersham, and partially because it freed me to take tea at the Castle Pub.

"What ho, hindmost." I greeted Ivor as he descended the stairs to the bar room, where I had already established a beachhead by the cold beef and stilton pie. "Try the butter-grilled lake trout. Odd tells me they were caught this morning by skilled and loving hands."

"They were." Ivor held up one skilled and loving hand while the other dished chilled French beans and buttery fillets of lake trout. "I was up at five."

"You reveal hidden depths, Inspector," I said with sincere admiration for the very particular sort of insanity that causes men to rise before the sun. "Is the trick to sneak up on the fish while they're still drowsy? I know that would work on me."

"Odd put me onto a lake upriver, the other side of the hill." Ivor inflated his lungs as though about to break into song. "I may just move up here, one day."

"You'd go mad, Inspector, pining for the bustle and Boisjolys of London." I shifted the tea, mustard and chutney pots to the next table to accommodate Ivor's feed pale. "Happily, only one of us was rousing lake trout from their beds while the other made headway in the case."

"I'm waiting for Blewit to return from Chesterfield," said Ivor conversationally. "Got it all figured out then, have you?"

"Not as such," I said. "I have, however, managed to complicate the situation further. There have been no less than two more crimes in your absence."

"Two?" Ivor was satisfyingly exasperated.

"Possibly more. Two that I know of. Tea?" I filled Ivor's cup and topped up my own. "In fact, let's say three, to play the odds."

"What is the nature of these crimes?" Ivor said 'crimes' as though one of us had been abusing the policeman's lexicon.

"They share many characteristics," I said. "Amulets, pilfering, and locked rooms, to name three."

"Locked rooms?"

"I know what you're thinking. Indeed, I was thinking the exact same thing — good thing Anty Boisjoly is on hand."

"That's not what I was thinking."

"It'll come to you. You've had a tiring day." I set aside my plate and made a focal point of my teacup. "Bunty and Sid —

78

Mrs Stokely and Cressida Carnaby, to you — both have revoltingly ugly amulets, provided as part of the broader curse-control service. This morning, both of them were stolen, according to the ladies, from locked rooms."

"Someone else has a key," said Ivor, as though stating the obvious as, indeed, he was.

"Someone else does have a key," I confirmed. "Lint, the dissenting maid, has the only copy but she was among witnesses before, during, and after the thefts, and she had her key on her the entire time."

"Are these amulets worth anything?"

"Only if you put a value on human life, Inspector," I said. "And believe in witchcraft, of course. Bunty, at least, has been severely distressed by the loss. She thinks it's now only a matter of time before the Carnaby Castle Curse notices that she's defenceless."

"Is that the point, do you think?" Ivor said this in the tone of a prompt, something for me to consider while he addressed the more pressing trout issue.

"I'd say there's definitely a psychological aspect to the affair," I said. "Possibly a compulsive thief? It would certainly explain the third new mystery."

Ivor allowed the drama to build with admirable restraint. An observer might assume that he was entirely distracted by butter-grilled trout.

Finally he put aside his knife and fork, briefly but thoroughly cleaned his plate with a knob of bread, drew on his tea, and said, "What new mystery?"

"One which appears to point to the identity of the perpetrator of the first two," I said.

"Which is?"

"Me." I took an enigmatic sip of tea — two could play this admirable restraint game — before adding, "I found the amulets in my room."

"*Your* room?"

"Also locked, incidentally. And yet when I popped by on my way here, I found not only the two amulets, but a third amulet, a garnet on a silver strand, a tea ball shaped like a little teapot — I'm keeping that — and what may or may not be a gold chain from a pocket watch. Hard to tell without the pocket watch."

"Is this just some clumsy effort to distract from the murder?" pondered Ivor.

"Possibly," I allowed. "Or — a diabolically cunning psychological machination of gears within gears within gearboxes, each more crafty and canny than the next." I took a cagey sip of tea. "But, really, probably just some clumsy effort to distract from the murder."

"With you in the role of the mug," observed Ivor.

"I'm the obvious choice," I said. "Thanks to Carnaby, I'm perceived by the gallery as comic relief, a sort of slender and sober Falstaff."

"How is the culprit getting into the rooms?"

"This question has much played upon my mind. Handicapped as I am by an adult view of the nature of magic, I'm forced to conclude that access was gained via the door." I paused briefly to say, "Thank you, Odd," as our plates were removed and a fresh pot of tea laid on. "It's made me even more wary of the death-trap that is the Carnaby Castle guest room, and I don't mean to be caught unaware. I have taken measures."

"Measures?" repeatedly Ivor warily. "What sort of measures?"

"An artifice of my own design," I explained. "After locking my door, I slipped a roll of letter paper into the keyhole, and pushed it almost out the other side. Anyone entering my room will unknowingly push the tube of paper through. By simple analysis of the lock I shall determine, before entering, if a mad killer awaits within."

By the retiring standards of the Castle Pub, a commotion ensued at the door, and Constable Blewit blew in.

"Afternoon Inspector, Mister Boisjoly." The constable deftly doffed his helmet onto the sideboard and exchanged it for a plate which he held like the palette of an artist. Soon it was a masterpiece of trout, pie, beans, and buns. I timed his arrival to a perfect cup of tea.

"Any joy, Constable?" asked Ivor.

"Some," replied Blewit to a forkweight of trout. "The post office was able to quite unmistakingly describe Wurt Carnaby, the butler, as the party what sent the telegram to London on the afternoon of the Tuesday before the Tuesday before last. The clerk expressed her doubts that Wurt would recall the occasion himself."

"Did she know Wurt by sight?" I asked.

"She was very descriptive."

"Yes, I daresay she was," I said. "There's something about the man's patina that calls out to one's inner poet."

"She was quite eloquent, yes sir," confirmed Blewit. "She's also familiar with Wurt — once every quarter or so he brings and receives castle mail in Chesterfield. She'd seen him most recently at Christmas, asleep in a snowbank."

"So, effectively, we know that someone from the castle sent the telegram to Carnaby at the Juniper, but we can't know who," I concluded. "Might even have been Wurt himself."

"It's as expected," said Ivor. "And, as mentioned, I don't share your fascination with the authorship of telegrams. What about the victim?"

"I received a reply from the Registrar General in London." Blewit stored a knot of pie in his cheek while he sourced his notebook and opened it on the table. "Ludovica Carnaby, née Ludovica Gaggiano..." which Blewit pronounced 'Gaggy-anno' "...formerly Ludovica Trewsbury, formerly Ludovica Birkit, was from Italy — town called Bergamo."

"Lovely people," I recalled. "Stunning mediaeval architecture, in particular you don't want to miss the basilica. Nor the risotto, while you're there — maybe a little rich for the English palate, but I have a congenital tolerance for saffron."

Blewit and Ivor regarded me with guarded interest.

"No casino to speak of," I concluded.

"What became of Trewsbury and Birkit?" asked Ivor.

"Ludovica's first husband was considerably older than she was," answered Blewit, euphemistically. "Bredon Birkit was sixty-eight when he died of heart failure in 1926. Of Sylvanus Trewsbury less is known. They were married — also in 1926 — and Ludovica was granted a divorce in absentia only last year."

"Must have been a whirlwind romance she enjoyed with Cecil," I observed.

"By all accounts it was," agreed the Constable. "They met in Milan..." Blewit paused while he and Ivor turned expectantly toward me.

"Well, it's Milan," I said. "Everyone knows Milan."

"They met in Milan at Christmas," continued Blewit, "and married there. They lived for some time in Ludovica's villa in Bergamo before coming to England. They registered the marriage on arrival in London three weeks ago."

"And then came to settle permanently in Hoy, bringing Cecil's years of merchant-marining and railway-budging to a warm, domestic finalé."

"But he must have known about the curse," opined Blewit. "Why would he have brought his bride here, of all places?"

"Cecil did not and, I think it's important to mention, *does* not believe in the curse," I said. "He thinks one of his family did in his wife."

The door opened again and we all turned to see Vickers step tenuously through, as though suspecting he had entered a private home by accident. He studied the interior of the pub and appeared to be nodding inwardly as he distinguished familiar landmarks — the stools and tables, Odd, the bar taps, the policemen and, finally, the old firm. I'd seen these symptoms in the past, most recently on a visit to Hamleys at Christmas when Vickers took a series of wrong turns and found himself in a display window that had been done up as the shrink-drink scene from Alice in Wonderland. He had to have a lengthy sit-down in the Mad Hatter's Tea Party window before I was able to convince him that he'd fit in a taxi.

"Don't stand on ceremony, Vickers," I said. "Pull up a hot cup of home. You look like you need it."

"Indeed, sir." Vickers installed himself across from Blewit as Odd descended with a fresh pot and cup.

When the clatter and steam subsided, Ivor renewed the interrogation of his constable.

"What about this Smith-Jones chap?"

"With the time and particulars to hand, Inspector, I was unable to conclusively confirm or deny his bona fides or lack thereof," said Blewit. "I don't know who Elwin Smith or Elwin Jones are."

"I know who he is," said Vickers, after swallowing what appeared the most restorative cup of tea since the Salamanca counter-offensive of 1812 predicated, unless I'm misinformed, on a single pot of Darjeeling.

"You do? Are you sure?" asked Ivor.

"Oh, yes, sir," said Vickers. "I wrote it down."

"How did you discover his real identity?" I asked.

"I saw his passport, among other private papers," said Vickers. "I was in his room."

"I say, Vickers, good show," I said, and then to Ivor, "It's the little misdemeanours, don't you think, that make amateurs so invaluable to an investigation."

"What were you doing in his room?" asked Ivor.

"You see, sir, my own room, here at this Castle Pub, is first on the right, top of the stairs."

"I think I can guess the rest," I said.

"Indeed, sir," confirmed Vickers. "I was at the other Castle Pub when I became prey, as I often am in the early afternoon, to a need to restore my reflexes. I retired to what I thought was my room and noticed that I appeared to have rather a lot of correspondence to get through, so I began looking through the papers on the desk."

"How long were you at this before realising where you were?" marvelled Ivor.

"In real terms, sir, I would say not more than half an hour, but I will get drowsy when reading."

"You took a nap," I surmised.

"It seemed the prudent course of action."

"In any case," said Ivor. "What did you discover?"

Vickers took another vital sip of tea and then searched his waistcoat pockets. He withdrew a fold of notepaper. "I learned the real name of the man calling himself Elwin Smith."

"And what is it?" asked Ivor.

"Sylvanus Elwin Trewsbury."

CHAPTER TEN

The Darkly Arbitrary Devil's Emissary

Obviously, somebody had to ferret the truth out of the newly christened Elwin Trewsbury. I proposed to Ivor that we draw straws or settle the issue with a quick brandy vintage recognition contest, and he countered with a proposal that I mind my own civilian business. I had matters to attend to at the castle in any case, as it happened.

The true and trusted tea-tracking talent which all Boisjolys can trace back to just after the Norman conquest led me to the library and a surprisingly complete collection of Castle Carnabys, all gathered around a harpsichord on which rested a silver platter and six tiny, perfect portions of Buxton pudding. Lint was distributing tea, in the moment I arrived, and Prax was watching proudly over her little flock at feeding. Carnaby, Nobby, Sid, Bunty, and Cecil were putting their share of pudding on their saucer and casting me resentful, hungry glances. Wurt was leaning on the mantelpiece, ceding to his malady from a flask.

"I suppose you'll want your share," said Cecil with all the warm welcome of a hole in the ice.

"Couldn't eat another speck," I said, holding up an 'oh, no, I couldn't possibly' hand.

"Have you had your tea, Anty?" asked Carnaby with agonisingly forced bonhomie.

"Eh?" I suppose, on reflection, I could have just said, yes, rather, proper knees-up it was, too, but that felt, in the moment, ungrateful for the hospitality that had been thus far inflicted upon me. "Memories of breakfast linger. I've been walking the grounds ever since, to keep it from clinging."

"There was barely a half a rasher each for breakfast," protested Cecil.

"And tea. With honey," I added. "Not to mention two shillings worth of unguent goes a very long way. I'll have one of those, though, Lint, just as it comes from the pot."

Lint handed over a steaming cup of simplicity and we all stood awkwardly facing one another over the harpsichord.

"What about my amulet, Mister Boisjoly?" asked Bunty in a sort of theatre whisper, as though she thought only I could hear her. "Have you found it?"

"Was I meant to be looking for it?"

"I assumed so, yes, the way you went off after learning how it went missing."

"A just assumption, Bunty — we Boisjolys tend to exude chivalry, whether we mean to or not." I sipped my tea and held Bunty's searching eye. "I haven't been looking for your amulet, Bunty, because I know what happened to it."

All eyes turned to Carnaby.

"Did you work out how the amulets were taken from locked rooms, Uncle Wselfwulf?" asked Sid.

"It was witchcraft, wasn't it Wself?" presumed Bunty.

"No, not as such," I said. "More of an emissary of dark forces, wouldn't you say, Wself?"

"Ehm, yes," agreed Carnaby. "Yes, this is precisely how I'd put it, I think."

"Emissary?" queried Bunty.

"A crow, to be precise," I said. "Buns the crow, as do most furred or feathered fellows, has taken a liking to me, and has observed me clinging to curtain chains, climbing bannisters formed of chain, and suspending a little jar of tar around my neck by, you'll never guess, a chain. He quite understandably drew the conclusion that I was fond of chains."

"You're drunk," said Cecil, as flat, objective commentary in passing.

"He's not." Bunty appraised me with wide eyes and spoke once again in her stage whisper, this time for Cecil's ears only. "He's touched."

"I dispute neither proposition. Nevertheless, it was a crow who spirited the amulets from your rooms, along with a number of other treasures, all of which are now on the mantelpiece in my room." I sipped my tea with cool aplomb. "They are gifts from a dear friend, you understand, and I regard them as such, but I shall return them in due course. Apart from the tea ball — I think I may have misplaced that."

"I must have my amulet, Mister Boisjoly." Bunty rattled her teacup to the harpsichord and urged me toward the door.

"I haven't had my tea," I pointed out. "How about I bring it to your room, later?"

"Please don't be long," implored Bunty, and then slipped out the door.

"You can drop mine off at my room whenever you please, Anty," said Cressida, slithering past me and sliding a cold hand up my arm and over my shoulder where it inspired a small *frisson* of fear. Then she, too, was gone.

By and by the Castle Carnabys finished their tea and sliver of Buxton pudding and then I was alone with Cecil.

"A crow," scoffed Cecil. "A likely story."

"Is it?" I asked. "I thought it was quite singular. I don't know many crows, mind you. Knew a Myna bird, once, that stole raisins right out of the scones, bold as you please. That was largely a partisan exercise, though, compared to the commerce in comradery of Buns the crow, and the Myna bird would only turn to crime when Carnaby was serving tea."

"How's that?"

"The bird was a guest at my club, in a manner of speaking. We were hosting him for Gasper Frisby while he settled a domestic issue involving a cat gifted to Mrs Frisby by her mother," I recalled. "It was the practice of one of our more puckish members — in the interest of a frank retelling, me — to give the poor thing its freedom most afternoons. Livened up teatime beyond all expectation."

"No, I mean, who's this Carnaby you said that serves tea in your club?"

"Did I say that?"

"You did."

"You're not thinking of Gasper Frisby?" I distracted. "Sounds rather like Carnaby, if you're not fully on your toes."

"Before that," insisted Cecil.

"Myna bird?"

"You said that you released the bird whenever Carnaby was serving tea."

"Yes."

"Well?"

"You object to my skylarking in a gentleman's club," I inferred. "Doubtless you're right. In my defence I'll note that this was way back in, I believe, March. We excuse the joys of boys, or all grown men condemn."

"What is that? Shakespeare?"

"Beermat."

"Isn't my cousin Wselfwulf a member of your club?"

"Practically a pillar of the place," I paltered, I contend, innocently with the truth.

"So what's he doing serving the tea?" Cecil popped his fragment of pudding into his mouth in a manner that made the act appear like a minor but flawless victory.

"Well, just, custom, what?" I equivocated. "Convention. Tradition. Those countless deeds and dictums that separate us from the beasts of the field, many of whom don't even drink tea."

"You're saying it's customary for members to serve tea at your club?"

"To each according to his needs, from each according to his abilities," I quoted. "The Juniper is a very progressive club. Do you know it?"

"No."

"Very, very progressive. Practically revolutionary."

"Better than this idle coagulation, I suppose." Cecil adjourned the inquisition with a sip of tea. "Not a one of them have worked a day for the luxury they take for granted."

"You don't object to Castle Carnabys turning their hand to honest toil, then."

"I should say not," said Cecil. "Do all of them a world of good, like it did me. I've shovelled coal, shovelled dirt and rocks — you wouldn't believe some of the things I've shovelled — hard work gives a man true worth."

"You're preaching to the converted, Mister Carnaby," I said as to a comrade. "Nothing more satisfying than really putting your back into a tea tray and multi-tiered sandwich stand."

"Pah," scorned the patriarch.

"Pah?"

"Just so, pah!" confirmed Cecil. "Probably don't know which end of a shovel goes where."

"I think so. The principle's not so very different from a caviar spoon, is it?"

"Pah," expelled Cecil, in a return to his core line of argument. "The real value of money is in having earned it."

"I'm sure you're right, in the main," I conceded. "Handy stuff to just have about the house, mind you, on a rainy afternoon or simply when planning a sabbatical in Monte Carlo."

"You don't have to tell me, Boisjoly, I've got the stuff in buckets." Cecil emphasised 'buckets' with a thump on the harpsichord that caused it to resonate an inquisitive 'hmmm?' "You know why?"

"Shovelling?" I divined.

"That's right, shovelling." Cecil raised a decisive teacup, but then thought better of it. "Well, no, not just shovelling. A man works his way up. Seizes opportunity. Takes chances." The shoveler's spirit soared on this testament but then hit something unyielding about ceiling height and dropped back to teacup level. "It's what drew my dear Ludovica to me."

People say they're not good at responding to grief as though it's a talent most everyone else has, like breathing in through one's nose and out through one's mouth, when in fact it's about as common as being able to breathe in through one's nose and out through one's mouth underwater. I present, as an anecdotal case in point, what I said next.

"What made you decide to bring your bride to Hoy, what with everything, and whatnot?"

"Why shouldn't I have?" Cecil dispensed with melancholy and returned to a more natural state of unaffected indignation. "How was I meant to know the place was infested with thieves and murderers? Last time I was here they were all just skivers and parasites."

"I will always marvel at the transformative power of raw ambition."

"Pah."

"Talking of vaulting ambition o'rleaping itself," I said. "I understand you know my mountain-climbing friend Elwin."

"You don't climb mountains."

"I don't climb mountains with a devoted passion," I acknowledged. "I merely meant that Elwin, who does climb mountains, is a mutual friend."

"No friend of mine," claimed Cecil. "Not if you're talking about that blustering windbag I met in the cemetery the day Ludovica died. He said his name was Elwin — *'Call me Win'*, the very idea."

"Turns out that was not only the day but the hour and minute — you and Elwin alibi one another for the very instant in question."

"Alibi?" Cecil spoke the word as though he found it simultaneously mystifying and deeply offensive. "Why should I want an alibi? For that matter, why should this Smith gasbag need one? What cause would he have to murder my wife?"

"None widely known, but I understand his very presence in town has drawn the interest of the authorities."

"Says he's researching his genealogy. Wants to prove he's a Town Carnaby." Cecil looked up with a renewed quizzical countenance. "That's dodgy as found fish, now I think of it."

"And until last Friday you'd never set eyes on the man? Quite sure?" I asked. "He's not lingering with murderous intent in the background of your wedding photographs, or a dangerous but charming rogue from your wife's past?"

"If you've got something to say, Boisjoly, I wish you'd come out and say it."

"Now, with that view, Mister Carnaby, you take your place among a very comfortable majority," I said. "I'm actually not entirely sure that I'm saying anything at all. Just pursuing a hunch."

"A hunch…" Cecil seemed to consider the word as something new and yet unshovelled.

"Do I hear the ringing of a distant bell?" I asked.

"Just… maybe something he said." Cecil glowered at a curious point in the middle distance, and in the next instant appeared to recall that I was in the room. "You're awfully nosy for a free-loading housepest. I thought Wselfwulf was the amateur snoop."

"Quite famously so, yes," I confirmed. "Doubtless Scotland Yard would put him up for a medal or some choice item from the King's birthday honour's list — or just stand him a drink, once in a new moon — but of course they can't be seen to openly encourage the competition. Wheels within wheels, and whatnot, what?"

Cecil levelled a flat, insouciant eye on me, as on an object in which he was rapidly losing interest.

"And what's it to do with you?"

"Oh, well, Wselfwulf and I are members of the same club, don't you know," I explained. "Never a brother's business unexplored. It's the Juniper motto. Or it would be, I expect, if it weren't already *'In mari meri miri mori muri necesse est'*."

Cecil's disinterested dial brightened with the subtle sort of smile that our nation's gargoyle carvers struggle so hard to reproduce.

"I don't know your club, Boisjoly," he said. "But I have heard of it."

"Oh, yes? Only in glowing terms, I've little doubt."

"Indeed. When my wife and I returned to England we enjoyed a brief honeymoon in London. We took a floor in Chelsea."

"Lovely quarter. Neighbourly, I think you'd call it, if you'd never been."

"We engaged a parlour maid for the duration. She came with references."

"Very wise," I commended. "You don't want to end up with a parlour maid who knows nothing about parling."

"One of them rather stood out among the rest," oozed Cecil. "It was signed by none other than Wselfwulf Carnaby, head steward of the Juniper Gentleman's Club."

❧

There was little I could do to salvage Carnaby's reputation with a man who regarded the both of us as what we incontestably were — shiftless shovel-shirkers. I resolved, therefore, to maintain my own rigorous standards and return the property innocently pilfered on my behalf.

The ingenuity of my countermeasure against mad killers hiding in my room, having been already briefly touched upon, is mentioned now only to explain why I stooped to examine the keyhole. Invisible to anyone but its architect, the roll of paper was still in place and the coast, consequently, clear.

"Hullo Buns, me old necklace nicker," I said to Buns, whom I surprised in the act of dropping off a length of copper wire. He fluttered from the balcony and lay his offering in military alignment with the two amulets, the garnet on a silver strand, teapot-shaped tea ball on a chain, and what may or may not have been a gold chain from a pocket watch. I added a tharf cake specially preserved from breakfast, and our transaction was complete.

"So, it *was* you," I said. "That's a happy coincidence. You'll forgive the presumption, I'm sure. I got the idea from a raven that lived in an oak tree above Gloucester gardens, where my father would often go to avoid my mother's judgmental eye. After a commerce of breadcrumbs and brief observation of Papa's habits, the bird began bringing him corks from whisky bottles."

I examined the plunder on the mantelpiece and took up the amulets and then carefully toured the room. The walls and door were solid and guileless, and the balcony was accessible only by crow. I was left with only the fireplace.

It was a rustic, rocky sort of construction, roughed out of the tower wall hundreds of years ago and hundreds of years after the tower itself was built. The interior was, unsurprisingly, black with soot so the uneven bricks were almost indistinguishable from one another, but for a little misshapen one, near the bottom and near the right. This brick had come away from its neighbours, slightly. Possibly because it was recessed, and possibly not.

It turned out not. I pressed the brick and it receded further into the wall, some dull mechanism tripped, and the back wall of the fireplace swung like a door, because that's exactly what it was. The stone wall slid into the darkness with the satisfying rasp of stone over stone and mysteries revealed, and I was looking into a secret passage.

CHAPTER ELEVEN

What Lies in Wait Beyond the Graveyard Gate

The hidden staircase was much like any other hidden staircase one might see in a mediaeval castle tower — narrow, of course, and damp and dark. Scant light seeped through the spaces where the stones had parted ways, but I thought to bring along an oil lamp.

The stairs were steep — more like a ladder than stairs, in fact — and seemed to go on indefinitely. I felt sure that I had descended further than the height of the tower and, indeed, the oil lamp had become indispensable, when I came to a narrow, arched stone doorway. Beyond was blotting black from which came the cold breath of a deep, deep cavern and the otherworldly wheeze and woosh of underground rivers. I pushed cautiously through, the oil lamp, courageously, leading the way.

The rough, ageless walls were wet and reflective and my lamp light scintillated all about me. The space was vast, though, and the lamp was little, so I was only able to confirm that I was in a multi-layered series of stone, iron, and wooden catwalks and staircases fitted haphazardly into the walls of a natural cavern, at the bottom of which, a hundred feet below, a racing river crashed around stalagmites as high as dizziness itself and as sharp as a Boisjoly witticism. I stayed close to the wall.

The ledges were wide enough and they had rope barriers threaded through iron stanchions, but I soon recognised that for the trap it was. Here and there and then again over there, the ledge was cracked and brittle or fallen away altogether. This additionally rendered the bannisters deceptively unreliable. At one point, as I ascended a small set of steps, a stone newel shook loose, shivered briefly as though waving goodbye, and then dove backwards into the churning waters. I received its sacrifice as cautionary.

The ledges and catwalks and stairs, I soon realised, were not only for admiring the terror of the prehistoric cavern — they wove in and out of the hill, leaving and joining each other and, no doubt, other passages to all parts of the castle. I selected a doorway at random and proceeded into the darkness.

It was after some considerable and, largely, blind navigation that I exited the labyrinthic passage from behind a rotating shelf of books in the library. I had acquired an important insight into the internal workings of the castle, along with a lustrous coat of spiders' webs and a small but loyal entourage of spiders.

The library was empty, now, and dark. Evening was stealing over the windows and I estimated that the time was very close to the twilight hour when Ludovica had been seen to be taken up by the mists. The window to the south, therefore, would have been Wurt's panorama on the proceedings.

The library was on the third and top floor of the keep and hence from the window the castle wall presented as the horizon below the scarp. The long shadow of the neighbouring hill was in that moment darkening the scene and a dense fog slithered over the mossy edge like something alive and misty and hungry for human company.

Time ticked toward turnips, and I had much to discover and more to reveal. I swung the bookshelf back in place and left the room by the door.

❧

The bar room of the Towny Castle Pub was empty but for a gentle gentleman's gentleman, gently napping. I agreed the details of tea with Odd and stood aside while Vickers came to the light of his own accord — he's a man with an admirable capacity for the tactical snooze but if anything he's too capable — goes right under, like a man on ether, and there's no telling how he might interpret what he encounters on resurfacing. It's best to keep the lights low and stimulation to a minimum. I once made the mistake of jostling him awake in the library where he'd dozed off waiting for me to return from a fancy dress party I'd attended dressed as the Grim Reaper, complete with plywood scythe. We never speak of it and I pretend to have forgotten the marvellous confessions the poor man made in the frenzy of his final moments.

So I observed from the shadows as Odd clattered down the tea tray. Vickers roused with a characteristic moment of light panic, saw the tea things and said "Ah, thank you, Vickers," and I knew it was safe to approach.

"What ho, old kipper," I said in my club whisper as I slid into the chair opposite. "Seen any good secret passages lately? I ask because if you had it would be a coincidence for the ages."

"Good…" Vickers glanced at the darkened window of the pub. "…evening, sir. Secret passages?"

"Probably best described henceforth as 'hidden' passages," I said. "You know what a gossip I am."

"These are hidden within the castle walls, I take it."

"Partially. Mostly under, though. Honeycombed throughout the foundations. It's a wonder the whole castle hasn't collapsed into the hill like a startled soufflé."

"Of course." Vickers gazed quizzically on some revelation in the distant past.

"You appear disappointingly prepared for my revelation, Vickers," I observed. "Are secret passages more common than I thought?"

"Quite possibly." Vickers returned his attention to the tea. "But I was referring to the name of the town and, more particularly, the hill, 'Hoy Tor'. In early Anglo-Saxon this would translate as 'Hollow Hill'."

"I've always maintained a tactful silence on the question, Vickers," I said. "But now I have to ask — how old *are* you?"

"I was exposed to some of the rudiments of Old English whilst in service to your late grandfather, the pet political project of whom was to reintroduce the language as a bulwark against rebounding American culture," explained Vickers. "He took particular umbrage with what he called the scourge of Dixieland."

"That rings true," I recollected. "When I think of Granpapa it's only with affection, of course, but I recall him as a man of views as broad as piano wire. Talking of which, have you seen Inspector Wittersham in your mad dashes around the metropolis?"

"The inspector is at the Castle Castle Pub," said Vickers. "In conference with Mister Trewsbury."

"Still? Must be an interesting conversation. I look forward to weedling the details out of the inspector when he least expects it." I rose and Vickers tried to beat me to it. "As you were, Vickers. Enjoy your restorative and, when you see him, you must give the inspector an important message on my behalf — tell him I've solved the mystery of the murder in the mist."

᠁

A wispy, misty carpet of white reflected the moonlight from the floor of the graveyard. That very same moonlight was working in close collaboration with the mausoleums, headstones, statuary, and general masonry to throw into sharp relief seraphim, cherubim, thrones, and a host of pallid plaster Yoricks.

I toured the little streets of the postal district of the dead, with addresses demarcated by commencement and closing dates of columns of Carnabys in long-term pieds-à-terre. The jolly policy of strict segregation was observed here as it was in life and in a not dissimilar manner — Town Carnabys rested beneath simple marker stones, and Castle Carnabys saw out eternity from within stately sepulchres bearing the castle coat of arms. Nevertheless, there was a notable *rapprochement*, architecturally speaking, with the passing of time. Town tombs became less rudimentary, and Castle crypts less ornate — one less spire, for instance, or an iron grate where a previous generation got a depiction of the Ascension in stained glass, all the way down to a modest little cenotaph for the late Capricia Carnaby, the departure date on which indicated that the poor girl was no more than seventeen when the curse took an interest in her affairs.

But it was in the 'second death' of the catacomb where class distinctions crumbled and brother lay shoulder to toe with brother. Hoy cemetery was worryingly large for a town that size and rather ominously dense but it was still obliged to observe the practice of the second burial, in which the backlog is filed in the ossuary to make room for new customers.

A miniature, granite-walled chapel in the middle of the graveyard served as the entrance to the catacombs. Inside it was gloomy with the sepia light from dusty stained glass windows, but there was a lantern and a handy box of matches next to the doorway which descended into darkness and, by all appearances, something dreamed up by Dante.

Nevertheless I had an important issue to settle with the dark, narrow passages of Hoy, and so I lit the lamp, duly cracked my head against the top of the doorway, and began my descent into the Carnaby catacombs.

Catacombs are a peculiar thing to have popped up on the road of human progress. There's little reason to go down there, if you're planning on coming back up, and yet they're typically laid out like the archives of the British Museum, as though there's a chance there's something in stock you might require at any minute. The ancestors are stacked on efficiency-shelving and, in some of the more fanciful continental variants with a surplus of material kicked up by revolution and plague, arranged into delightful motifs of decidedly dubious taste.

This catacomb, however, was of your dignified, dour, sanctuary design. A serene and sombre snuggery where a body could expect to enjoy a good infinity's sleep undisturbed. There was a main hall — narrow and unsuitable for social gatherings or much of anything requiring headroom, but serviceable — and three or four guest wings. In short it had, as a catacomb, everything. There was even an atmospheric dank odour and accompanying clamminess to the chill, underground air.

All this catacomb lacked, if I were to take the liberty of criticising, was an emergency exit, or any sort of secondary access. I followed the corridor to the end where it was a solid wall of rough stone which, I note for later significance, was wet. Indeed, a trickle of river water started at a little natural spout about shoulder height and wriggled its way to the floor, and had been doing so for long enough that it had worn itself a familiar path into the black sandstone.

This was all and more than I needed to know, but as I was making my farewells to the Carnaby ancestry a low boom echoed through the cavern. Low booms can mean a number of things, depending on where you are, but in the moment and in the catacomb I knew that it could mean only one thing — someone had closed the door.

I rested the lamp on the ground and dashed up the stairs and, in the darkness, ran directly into the heavy wood and iron door, which handily retained the heavyweight title. I was locked in and, only slightly more worryingly, I was deliberately locked in. I called out a dignified "Aaaaaaa! Help! Help! I'm locked in!" or something similarly redolent. Nothing. Not even an echo, just the dull, sound-absorbing silence of a sealed chamber.

Then my kerosene lamp flickered, choked, and died.

There's no darkness like complete darkness. The full, frontierless nothing that is an underground cavern with a fine, well-fitted door firmly in its frame, narrows to nothing the distinction between eyes wide open and having been knocked unconscious with a brick. It's a close, clingy darkness, too. Right in front of your eyes, in fact, and hence not a little confining.

I shuffled back down the stone stairs and felt about on the floor for the lamp. I couldn't find it and the fact that it was probably inches away failed to amuse me, in the moment. I rose and endeavoured to retrace my steps which, in that sort of darkness, is the hard side of impossible. I did find the lamp, however, and also kicked it over and broke it. Tie result, effectively, because the matches, I then recalled, were still on the other side of the door.

In a manner of speaking, I'd been prepared for this moment for years since my father selected Poe's *The Cask of Amontillado* to read to me as a bedtime story in an ultimately successful effort to never be asked again. Without spoiling the story, it left me with a dread of immurement similar — and, it turns out, equally rational — to my fear of heights. The plan was always, in broad strokes, to experience panic, dizziness, and shortness of breath, and I evolved the strategy in the moment to have a piercingly loud emotional breakdown at the door, where it would be of most use.

I moved toward the stairs and walked flat-faced into a wall. In my scramble for the lamp I must have turned myself around. I determined to slide along the wall, in the tradition of the mathematical problem of the drunk in the maze, until I again had my bearings. Within minutes the method bore fruit and I was hopelessly lost. Where I was sure to encounter stairs I met another wall, perpendicular to that which I was following and formed of raw Carnaby forebear. I tamped down the panic with the certitude that the catacombs were exactly as they had been when I had a lamp and they were not, in spite of all evidence to the contrary, closing in on me.

Doubtless I'd navigated into one of the secondary corridors, and only needed to persist and I'd come out the other side. Then my hands were wet, and then I hit another perpendicular wall, then there were walls all around me, and then I began to believe in ghosts.

There's a fatalism that comes over me — when I'm dangling off cliff sides or buried in crypts — that thinks what's needed most at times of existential dread is about an ounce and a half more of the same. So it was that in this darkest moment and darker corner my mind went back to *The Cask of Amontillado,* which I read again as an adult to discover that my father had given the tale his own, paternal twist. The original story is grim enough and ends with a chap bricked into a wall, but Papa told it in the first person of Montresor who, too drunk to tell which side of the wall was which, wound up entombing himself. There the story ended, but for an epilogue added by my father, told from the perspective of the intended victim.

I imagined Vickers narrating what he supposed to be my final hours, probably confusing me for my father or forgetting whether or not I'd accompanied him to Hoy. Or perhaps Ivor, after piecing together that which I had already concluded with regards the fate of Mrs Ludovica Carnaby, would add the discovery of my remains as a grim adjunct to his official report, which would then be serialised in the Times. Worse still, it would likely be whoever it was that had locked me in this living tomb that would recount some self-serving version of the final chapter of the life of Anty Boisjoly.

As I reflected on my assassin, a distinctive footfall came to my ears. Possibly my hearing had increased in sensitivity to compensate for total blindness, and what I was hearing was the fall of a distant leaf onto a patch of long grass. Perhaps, when the door was closed, whoever closed it was on the inside. Or it may have been the skeletal remains of some ancient Carnaby, seizing this opportunity to redress some bygone grievance against the living. I was in a state of mind open to a range of contingencies.

And there it was again. This time it was more of a skittering, scratching, scrabble across the stone floor and I didn't so much hear it as feel it as a series of tremors down my spine. I reminded myself that whoever was in here with me had no greater visibility than I. Of course, there's no telling what senses may be at the disposal of the undead.

I confess that panic began to overtake me, and when I sensed a distinct movement in the air about my left ear I felt the fear slice through my heart, then take a sharp turn to my liver, ripple down my leg and dash off into the night, screaming like a banshee's voice coach. With no real strategy, I acted. If this was to be the end of Anty Boisjoly, it wasn't going to be for want of running and shrieking, and that's precisely what I did.

And then something hard and harsh hurtled at my head and brought it all to a close.

CHAPTER TWELVE

Purgatory's Category of Vainglory Allegory

It seems entirely obvious, now I think of it, that of the seven terraces of purgatory the one into which Dante would bung the gluttonous would be in every way exactly like the Carnaby catacombs. I certainly couldn't mount much of a defence accused of at least one other deadly sin — sloth, comes slowly to mind — but it only stands to reason that I would await judgement in a damp cellar without so much as a serviceable gin. Even Poe's Fortunato had his snootful of Amontillado to take the edge off being bricked into a wall.

I'm not going to tell Dante his business. For all I know I had been given what passes for very roomy quarters in the gluttony wing of purgatory, but as near as I could tell in the more-than-total darkness, I had been bricked into a cell the rough dimensions of the telephone box at Burlington House. Not built for capacity, those telephone boxes, although I did once squeeze four other Junipers and myself into one at Paddington Station, for reasons which seemed, at the time, spiffing, but have since escaped me. I rely on my biographers to recall that, while he held a hard line on mixed cocktails, Anthony Boisjoly was always up for a lark.

I deduced that someone with exceptional night-vision, a grudge, and a stout length of wood had stunned me long enough to enclose me within the walls of the catacomb. According to my experience with masonry, this could have taken anything from twenty minutes to the rest of the season, but all four walls felt as solid as if they'd been standing unchanged for a century.

Musing on my limited options, a suggestion came to me through blank space. A whispered voice taunted me in the darkness, suggesting that I should "claw".

"It may come to that," I admitted to the void, "but I'll wager you unto half my kingdom that it would be appreciably quicker if you'd just call for help."

The voice only repeated "claw" with calm temerity, and in the instant I recognised the advice not as "claw" but "caw". On its own and as advice, 'caw' wasn't of considerably greater utility than 'claw' but it wasn't advice — it was a beacon.

"Is that you, Buns old man?"

"Yaw," he replied in the affirmative, and I felt a wave of hope wash over me commensurate with the depths of despair into which I'd descended. Buns' call was coming from a direction, a geometric point in my heretofore mono-dimensional existence.

"Buns, say that again."

"Caw?"

"Yes, that. It definitely bears repeating."

Buns called out again and again, and I moved sightlessly toward him. Soon I realised that what I'd taken for an enclosed cell was a complicated fold of walls into which I'd somehow wandered in the dark. I negotiated a narrow passage and the call of caw grew louder and clearer and more distinctly positional. I followed Buns' aria like a lodestar and within minutes I felt cool, damp, delightful night air and, lo, I saw a misty slip of moonlight.

I fumbled up a narrow flight of stairs and came to a mouldy old door, quite manageable compared to that which until only recently had stood between me and a lifetime of service to my fellow man, composing witty telegrams and subsidising the British bookmaking industry.

With several stuttering scrapes and shuddering shoves, I opened a low door into a tiny crypt, like the tip top of a belfry. Cosy, is the word I might employ, if I hadn't had all the enclosed spaces I needed for approximately ever. The moon was filtered through stained-glass windows on three walls, illuminating most theatrically an altar on which some dark ceremony appeared to have been recently performed. The bones of some unfortunate bird were arranged on an oilcloth, a thick church candle had burned to a molten blob, and two pewter chalices, stained with something scarlet, glimmered in the moonlight.

"Awd!" diagnosed Buns. He was just outside the crypt, perched on the head of a concrete Gabriel, framed by a full moon.

"Most intriguing, indeed," I agreed. "We'll add it to the list of grist and grievances. In the meantime, though, I don't mind saying that I'm feeling more than a little persecuted."

"Aw," sympathised Buns.

"Your concern for my well-being is appreciated, Buns old lifesaver, though not as much, obviously, as is your role in preserving it."

"Tawk," dismissed the crow, modestly.

"It isn't just talk," I countered. "I mean it most heartily. I'll settle up with you properly in a moment and manner more fitting. Nearer term, though, what I need is a spiritual restorative."

"Scawtch!"

"Exactly what I had in mind," I said. "Let's hope that one of the Castle Pubs keeps witching hours."

The Castle Castle Pub was, thankfully, still open for trade. I had no idea, in the moment, if that was peculiar or not — it might have been early morning, days had possibly passed since I was last seen. I wondered if Baldwin was still Prime Minister.

There was even some boisterous custom scattered about the place, in the form of what looked like a travelling salesman and a matching pair of vicars, and a roundtable with Hoy's entire inventory of constables, valets, and inspectors from Scotland

Yard. I organised an undiluted large one from Wandalen at the bar and stealthily approached.

"What ho, search party," I said, breaking the happy news that Anty Boisjoly still lived.

"Evening Boisjoly," Ivor glanced up from his pint, back down, and then back up again. "What have you done to your head?"

"Noticeable, is it?" I put a hand to the extrusion and encountered embedded grit and a dull ache.

"You look like you walked into a stone wall."

"Precisely the look I was aiming for," I said. "That's what happened. I've been unconscious in the catacombs since, I assume, yesterday. What time is it?"

"Eight o'clock," answered Blewit. "Mister Vickers here said he saw you only an hour ago."

"It's only been an hour?" I slid onto the bench where Ivor made space. "This explains why you weren't looking for me."

"Yes, that would be the reason," agreed Ivor, distractedly. "Do you want to know about this Elwin Trewsbury affectation?"

I was employed, in the moment, in following that divine diffusion of whisky trickled liberally over hunger and fatigue. I allowed it to exalt its way in tingling tremors to my extremities, repairing, warming, and reassuring the sinews it encountered along the way. So, though I was bursting with solutions to impossible murders, I played along.

"He's Ludovica Carnaby's son," I surmised.

"What? How the devil did you work that out?" asked Ivor, with a pleasing pique that paired perfectly with the whisky. "He's older than she was."

"Stepson, I should have said," I corrected. "He's the son of Sylvanus Trewsbury, Ludovica's second husband."

"That's right," confirmed Ivor, with a slow and satisfying shake of the head. "Alright then, go on, you must be itching to say how you knew."

"In fact, I'd forgotten all about it, in light of everything else." With a subtle gesture I confirmed that my forehead was still attached. "I felt it unlikely that Win Jones would be Sylvanus Trewsbury because Ludovica wouldn't have been able to remarry with a living husband near at hand, and we know from Constable Blewit's investigations that the late Mrs Birkit-Trewsbury had a decided preference for the mature gentleman. Did he say what he was doing in Hoy?"

"You don't know?"

"I'm not a mind-reader, Inspector."

Ivor considered the prospect with a pensive swallow of Castle Castle bitter.

"He says he was hoping for a chance to speak to Ludovica..." Ivor put down his beer and looked meaningfully at me. "...alone."

"Because he wants to know what happened to his father," I concluded.

"He claims to know what happened to his father," said Ivor. "He says Ludovica killed him."

"He admitted a whacking great motive, just like that?"

"I may have caught him back-footed. I told him from the outset that Ludovica Carnaby had been murdered."

"He didn't know?" I asked.

"It would appear not," said Ivor. "He knew that there'd been a death — in fact he heard it from you — but assumed that it was a Castle Carnaby."

"So he told me," I recalled. "But he also told me that he once damaged a horse — it's hard to know what to believe. How does he think his father died?"

"He reckons Ludovica poisoned the old man, like Lucrezia Borgia." Ivor looked dubiously into his beer. "Says that's how she did in her previous husband, too, with some sort of plant toxin, the effects of which are indistinguishable from a heart attack."

"Diabolical, if true," I observed. "But if Ludovica had a magical cardiac-potion, why is Trewsbury Senior missing? She commits the perfect crime and doesn't even want credit? I'm beginning to suspect that Mister Trewsbury has never even met Lucrezia Borgia."

"The way Trewsbury tells it, she miscalculated," said Ivor. "He says his father's like him — big and busting and not so easily knocked off his perch by any leaf extract. Ludovica had to resort to plan B and biff the old man over the head with something, and probably drown him in the reflecting pool."

"Turning what had been an innocent heart attack into a gruesome murder," I surmised. "What Shakespeare might have described as 'gilding the lily', were he misquoting Shakespeare."

"Exactly."

"Anything to it, do you think?" I asked.

Ivor gestured to his second-in-command with a toast of his pint, and Blewit flipped back in time through his notebook.

"Mister and Mrs Trewsbury were living in a villa in Bergamo at the time of his disappearance, in a villa purchased by Mister Trewsbury only the previous year. According to Italian police, the staff had been given the night off..." Blewit looked meaningfully at the assembly. "...by Mrs Trewsbury, who says that her husband just packed his bags and left, without explanation. She believed, she said, that he planned to return to England, but there's no record of him having done so. In fact..." Again, Blewit gauged the room for the punchline. "...there's no further record of Sylvanus Trewsbury at all."

"So Elwin followed Ludovica to Hoy, ostensibly, to reminisce about his father," I concluded. "That rather imposes on credulity's good nature."

"It does," agreed Ivor. "He admits only that he wanted to persuade her to confess."

"He didn't strike me as a man with a mastery of the subtle art of diplomacy. Doubtless I missed it — our encounter was brief. Where is he now?"

Ivor and Blewit shared subtly different but equally dubious glances, Ivor's saying 'Shall I tell him?' and Blewit's expressing 'Yes, do.'

"He's gone," said Ivor, and retreated into his beer.

"Where?"

"London, I expect," said Ivor. "He packed his bags and left nearly an hour ago."

"You let him go?

"We had no cause to hold him — he has an unimpeachable alibi. Two alibis, in fact, if you count Cecil Carnaby, whom he saw in the cemetery some ten minutes after the murder, and Wandalen Kettle, who saw them both."

"Nevertheless, Inspector," I said. "I would have thought that, in light of what Vickers told you, you'd have exercised some small device from your considerable trunk of discretionary powers."

Ivor and Blewit turned their attention to Vickers, who was preoccupied with a brimming small ale. He peeked over the tankard and realised that he had some answering to do.

"Did I not communicate Mister Boisjoly's news, Inspector?"

"No, you didn't. What news?" asked Ivor.

"Most vexing." Vickers focussed his furrowed brow. "I feel sure I told someone."

"It might be useful to know who," I observed.

"Ah, well…" Vickers drew meditatively on his beer. "Mister Trewsbury, I believe. He was leaving the pub as I arrived, and I recollect asking him if he'd seen the inspector, for I had an important message to relay."

"Very well, you told Elwin. Anyone else?"

"Cecil Carnaby and Mrs Stokely," said Vickers tentatively. "Yes, I recall that she seemed very anxious, and I thought the news might bring her some comfort."

"To cut to the chase, Vickers, apart from the inspector here, is there anyone in Hoy you didn't tell?"

"Tell what?" exasperated Ivor.

"That I had solved the mystery of the mist," I said, sipping coyly on my whisky. "I know how it was done."

"Of course you do," said Ivor with that irate resignation that I regard among his signature charms. "And I suppose your explanation neatly exonerates your club steward."

"As it happens, no, it doesn't," I confessed.

"Well, there you are then." Ivor said this more to Blewit than to anyone else. "How did he do it?"

"He didn't."

"But you just said…"

"…that I know how it was done."

"But not who did it."

"Just so, not who did it."

"I beg to differ, Mister Boisjoly," differed Ivor. "You do yourself an injustice. The only viable suspect without an alibi is your Carnaby — if you've determined how he did it then you have, by extension, determined that he did."

"On the contrary, old contrarian," I differed right back. "No one, including Carnaby, has an alibi for the murder of Ludovica Carnaby, and what's more none of the eyewitnesses saw it."

"It was an accident, then," stated Blewit, with rhetorical relief.

"No, Constable, that's not what Mister Boisjoly is saying, is it, Mister Boisjoly?" said Ivor.

"I'm afraid not. Nor was it suicide," I said, anticipating the dubiously next best thing. "No, Ludovica Carnaby was murdered, but she wasn't killed by the mists or even a fall — she was bludgeoned to death at the bottom of the cliff, after climbing down of her own accord."

"But, the mists," protested Blewit. "Everyone saw her fetched up."

"They saw her step up," I corrected. "A small but vital distinction, given the appearance of a supernatural act by aid of a little mound of moss, over which one climbs to reach the steps or, going the other direction, the safety of solid ground. The mist in these parts and at that time of the evening, I've noticed, has a distinctly languorous quality. It's thick and heavy and it likes to lie close to the ground, creating the illusion that anyone stepping up onto a soft mound is being raised by the mists."

"But everyone said they saw her fetched up," pointed out Blewit.

"Precisely," I agreed, for I like to encourage audience participation. "Indeed, everyone had remarkably similar accounts of what they saw — is that sort of consistency typical of eyewitness statements in your experience?"

"Not at all," said Ivor, as a sort of admission.

"No," I said. "But the mist and the optical illusion and, above all, the influence of the myth of the curse, which everyone was already expecting to claim Ludovica Carnaby, created the vanishingly rare testimonial consensus."

"You don't mean to say it was auto-suggestion?"

"Of course it was. Don't underestimate the power of willful credulity." I stole a steadying sip of brown comfort before relaying the painful facts. "Only this morning I was able to face a paralysing fear of heights by putting my faith fleetingly but fully into a lucky charm. More recently still, I was prepared to believe that I had been entombed by and among the living dead. Still not sure I'm free of that particular delusion, entirely."

"But here are six people who all saw the same thing," pointed out Ivor.

"Exactly. Mass delusion is the most credible kind," I contended. "Working with an already very convincing illusion, each saw what they expected to see and/or what they'd been assured the others also saw. Same thing happened at the Juniper, once, when every single one of us had the most uncanny run of bad luck after the revels committee acquired a crate of pre-war whisky that, it was rumoured, had been illegally salvaged from a wreck on which all hands had perished. While those bottles were on the premises, not a one of us could pick a winner, umbrellas went missing at an alarming rate that couldn't be accounted for by the most improbable coincidence, members were constantly being locked out of their houses at night, and nearly half the enrollment — self included — was nicked for various offences on entirely unique and separate occasions. It soon became generally received that the whisky was cursed."

"You were all just looped on pre-war whisky," concluded Ivor.

"To the follicles." I smiled in nostalgic recollection. "Shows how these things can get started, though. Cribbage Digby wanted to call in an exorcist."

"Very well," said Ivor, as one whose interest in the psychology of the modern clubman had been satiated. "And how is it that you conclude that Mrs Carnaby was murdered at the bottom of the cliff?" asked Ivor.

"Elementary, Inspector. I determined that Ludovica Carnaby was killed at the bottom of the cliff because that's where the body was found, a mere ten minutes after she was seen, as we now realise, willingly going there. There's no other explanation that doesn't require believing in witches, curses and, by logical extension, the healing powers of liquorice root."

"Ten minutes isn't a lot of time," observed Ivor.

"It's not, I agree, but it's evidently enough, and in light of the scramble for assistance and safety that ensued in the castle immediately following the tragic event, almost anyone could have crossed the garden unseen and followed Ludovica down the steps."

"Very well," sighed Ivor. "Constable, we'll need to question everyone in the castle again, and determine where they were in the ten minutes following what we all assumed was the murder of Ludovica Carnaby, and above all who, if anyone, was seen leaving the castle."

"That would prove inconclusive, Inspector, at best," I said. "For the Carnaby Castle Cognoscenti, the place is a hive of hidden passages."

"You're not serious."

"Positively infested with the things. It's so one can hardly press a hidden, recessed brick in the back of a fireplace without falling into one."

"Do you know them?"

"Not intimately," I confessed. "I crossed from my room in the south tower to the library, but it was, in the main, a solitary experience."

"Could someone use these passages to go from the castle to the bottom of the scarp — and back — unseen?" asked Ivor.

"Possibly," I said. "I was pressed for time and didn't do a full land survey, but it's a theory that would doubtless repay close study. Let us review... immediately following what everyone supposed was the murder, Bunty made her way to the courtyard from the south tower..."

"And she saw Prax in the tower..." added Blewit.

"Did she? That's very interesting..." I said. "In the courtyard, Lint encountered Bunty, who then retired to the keep, but of course she could have left it via secret passage. Simultaneously, Wurt left the keep, and met Lint in the courtyard, and they were soon joined by Prax."

"How long is that?" asked Ivor.

"About seven minutes — Lint says that Prax arrived from the gatehouse about five minutes after she met Wurt in the courtyard," I said. "Prax had seen Cecil in the cemetery, and so they sent Wurt to fetch him."

"But he didn't show up," added Blewit.

"He probably got distracted by an inviting ditch. Or lost his balance," I speculated. "Or stopped for a top-up. The man's an Olympian in his field."

"Or he didn't get there in time," Blewit withdrew his constable's chronicle and opened it on the table. "Some ten minutes after sunset, when everyone says that Ludovica went over the side — Mister Cecil and Mister Trewsbury were in the Castle Castle Pub."

"So, Elwin Trewsbury and Cecil Carnaby have only each other as an alibi for the time of the murder," concluded Ivor.

"Not even," I said. "They didn't actually see each other until Elwin came out of the catacombs."

"But the cemetery is two miles uphill from the scarp," pointed out Blewit. "No one could have made it there and back in ten minutes."

"We know it was ten minutes then, do we?" I asked.

"Mister Barnaby, Prax the cook and Lint, the maid, gathered in the courtyard some five minutes after what they believed to be the death of Mrs Ludovica." Blewit turned to a pertinent page of his notebook. "They proceeded to the top of the scarp, from which they could make out a body on the rocks, some five minutes after that. Mister Barnaby and Lint descended and confirmed that Mrs Ludovica was deceased."

"Where was Sid?"

"Sid?"

"Cressida Carnaby," I explained. "I thought that she was with her brother on the allure."

"That's what she told us," confirmed Blewit. "But she remained on the wall when Mister Barnaby descended."

"Which leaves us with no suspects, again, unless there's a shortcut from the castle to the scarp — and back again — in which case, we have too many suspects," I said.

"Including and particularly Wselfwulf," added Ivor.

"If you insist," I allowed. "And, clearly, you do."

"I'm afraid that I don't have the benefit of your gentlemen's club blinkers," confessed Ivor. "So I'm forced to draw my conclusions from the evidence at hand which, according to you, means that unless there's a secret passage leading from the castle to the bottom of the scarp, your club steward is still the only one who could have murdered Ludovica Carnaby."

I felt duty-bound to return to the castle before the rozzers, and so I dined quickly and efficiently on cold steak and mushroom pie, a pickled onion, egg and stilton on oatcakes, two small house ales and a square of ginger parkin. The fare at the Castle Castle Pub was uncannily and even suspiciously similar to that of its nearest competitor in the Castle Pub game, and so I exercised restraint.

By happy coincidence I fell into stride with Prax Carnaby, the overqualified cook, who was coming out of the graveyard as I left the pub.

"Good evening, Mister Boisjoly." Prax smiled that vaguely knowing smile that, on me, I'm told can present as smug. On her it merely appeared knowing.

"Hullo, Chef. Fraternising with the forebears?"

"Picking mushrooms." Prax held up a basket of tawny toadstools. "Late evening is the best time."

"I thought you might have been paying your respects to poor Capricia Carnaby."

"Capricia Carnaby?" Prax looked vaguely back toward the graveyard, now being swallowed by the fog. "Why would I be doing that?"

"Why indeed?" I agreed. "After all, Capricia Carnaby isn't dead, are you?"

CHAPTER THIRTEEN

Loftis' Lonely Lot in Life

Prax studied me in a manner in which I've been studied many times.

"You're wondering if I'm bluffing," I surmised. "Shall I tell you how I know that you're really Capricia Carnaby?"

"I think you'd better."

"The amulet," I said.

"I thought that might have had something to do with it," sighed Prax. "Anything else I should watch out for in future, assuming you're not going to give me away?"

"Only over-educated swots with an eye for anomaly. Know any?"

"Just the one."

"Then your secret is safe," I assured her. "Although I'll add that I might have overlooked the fact that there were three amulets and, therefore, three Castle Carnaby women on the premises, had you not taken yours back, using the secret passage."

"You know about that, too, do you?"

"I do, and for the same reason — on the day of the murder, you say that you saw everything from the north tower, and minutes later you were able to identify Cecil Carnaby in the cemetery. The only view from the castle which gives onto the cemetery is my balcony in the south tower, and you somehow achieved that without being seen. Meanwhile, Cressida was on the wall, Lint and company were in the courtyard. These are the only two ways to access the south tower, except for what must have been a third way. Obviously, that's also how you recovered your amulet."

"That doesn't explain how you reckoned that I'm Capricia."

"No, I confess, that's me playing the odds — first, of course, there's the fact that Capricia doesn't have a tombstone nor a crypt. Instead there's a cenotaph, from the Greek 'kenos', meaning empty, and 'taphos' meaning tomb. There was no body and discarding, as I do, the theory that Capricia Carnaby was fetched up — and remained up — by cursed mists, I resort to the less fanciful explanation that she simply climbed down the cliff and ran away, to avoid an arranged marriage with her famously unappealing cousin, Loftis, from the Norse, 'Lauft', meaning 'smells like the floor of a barn.'"

"He did, too."

"I'm joking. It doesn't mean that," I confessed. "Rather, it might do, but it would be a huge and delightful coincidence. In any case, you managed to resist the allure of a life with Loftis Carnaby and the glittering temptations of the metropolis of Hoy."

"Somehow, yes," said Prax. "Half the town was expecting me to be claimed by the curse, and as the wedding day approached I was toying with the idea of throwing myself off the scarp anyway."

"It would have been an irreplaceable loss to gastronomy."

"Thanks. Anyway, in a moment of inspiration I had a better idea — the fog was rolling over the side of the scarp, there was a little boat at the pier, I had a stack of wedding dosh on me..."

"A perfect confluence of circumstance."

"I looked back at the wedding party, in particular Loftis who happened, in that moment, to have caught a brisk upwind, and I stepped up onto the mound, all floaty-like, as though I was being carried off. Then I dropped down onto the steps and into the fog."

"Most cinematic," I said. "And they all bought it, just like that."

"Of course. It's what most of them expected to see happen anyway, and a good share of them would have been disappointed if it hadn't."

"They didn't come looking for you?"

"Probably," guessed Prax. "If only for form's sake — there was a wedding planned, after all — but I was long gone."

"In a boat, you say."

"Yes. The river runs fast from here to the bottom of the hill. Why?"

"Oh, just an idle fancy — I like to think of you hiding in the secret passage until nightfall, then making your escape disguised as a Berber spice merchant."

"How was I meant to have hidden in the secret passage?"

"By way of the hidden access at the bottom of the scarp."

"There is no hidden access at the bottom of the scarp."

"Quite sure?" I asked. "You'd make a fetching Berber."

"Quite sure. The passages were carved out of natural caverns, well above the waterline and only just underneath the castle, maybe a hundred feet above the river and countless sharp, brittle stalagmites."

"Convincing," I opined. "Disappointing, but conclusive."

"Why is it so important to you there should be an entrance to the passage at the bottom of the scarp?"

"It's not for me, so much," I confessed. "I'm enquiring on behalf of a friend. Poor Inspector Wittersham is so at a loss for suspects in the case of the unfortunate Ludovica Carnaby that he's taken to persecuting lake trout."

"I thought your fellow clubman Wselfwulf was the amateur detective." Prax said this with a wry, indulgent sort of tone, as though 'fellow clubman' was herein synonymous with 'imaginary friend'.

"I'm functioning as a sort of deputy," I claimed. "I have studied his methods extensively — they amount to a floating ratio of intuition and trenchant social commentary, through the lens of a quality education."

"That so."

"T'is."

Prax had stopped walking now and was smiling at me in the darkness.

"Your club holds its stewards to a high standard then."

"Ah," I said, for it seemed the right thing to say. "You knew about that, did you?"

"Mostly," said Prax. "I knew that Wselfwulf was in service, in some capacity. I only just now received confirmation that he was a steward at the Juniper."

"Well played," I said. "Head steward, for the record, and probably the finest in London. How did you work it out?"

"Just bearing, mainly," mused Prax. "I've seen a lot of the world and the different types who inhabit it. Wselfwulf is intuitively scrupulous. Terrible actor, though. Not as plainly transparent as you, obviously. Wselfwulf, at least, manages to call you Anty. You can't help but refer to him as 'Carnaby' in exactly the tone of one who's always heard 'yes, sir' in reply."

"The curse of privilege," I explained. "Don't know how I bear up, some days. Talking of which, while I admire you both for it very much, you're Castle Carnabys, why don't you just assume your place among the idle classes?"

"I can't answer for Wselfwulf, but in my case I'm too fond of eating. As a castle domestic, I get a paltry wage and a roof over my head. As a resident I'd get the roof, probably in a draughty tower."

"I was under the impression that until Cecil's recent return, Carnaby was castle despot," I said. "Am I to understand that he's a miser? I don't like to speak ill..." I looked up and down the empty street before speaking ill, "...but the man's never overpoured a drink in his life."

"He might be, I couldn't say," said Prax. "He tried to sell a couple of castle properties in town, I believe, but was legally prevented."

"Yes. Inspector Wittersham tells me that only the eldest living descendent of Ranulph Carnaby holds executive power, and even that's limited to maintenance, upkeep and persecuting witches."

"Then why does your inspector think that Wselfwulf murdered Ludovica?"

"Rather an athletic leap, that," I observed.

"It's true though, isn't it?" Prax resumed walking toward the castle and I resumed walking next to her. "It's why you're so anxious to widen the gallery of suspects."

"Partially, I confess," I said. "And in equal measure I regard it as a sort of civic duty to complicate the life of Inspector Wittersham. He's a stout defender of the creative dialectic."

"Wish I could help," said Prax. "But the only way to the bottom of the scarp — apart from a dead drop onto jagged rocks — is the stairs."

※

At the castle Prax proceeded to the kitchen to, I expect, slice mushrooms into a transparent film with a straight razor, and I climbed unsteadily to my room to bathe my head and feel sorry for myself. Time was at a premium, though, so in the end I quickly washed up, changed into something inquisitive, had a quick brood, and in two shakes of a sheep's extremities I was ready to face any two men capable of locking a London gadabout in a Hoy catacomb.

The first prospect I encountered was Wurt, who I found leaning against an interior buttress of the gatehouse, gazing sceptically at the moon.

"Hello Wurt, old spurt," I greeted. "You look fully brimmed."

And he did. There's something unmistakable about two eyes operating independently.

"Evening, Mister Boisjoly," said Wurt, orienting largely by sense of sound. "Oh, indeed, sir. I'm most afflicted tonight. Most afflicted." He shook his head reproachfully at the fates. "It's all the activity, you understand. Visitors at all hours, demanding rooms and expecting great shipments of luggage delivered up all manner of stairs. It takes its toll, Mister Boisjoly, and leaves a strong man defenceless."

Wurt illustrated the point with an inexorable draw from his flask.

"Visitors, Wurt?" I asked. "Big chap, by any chance? With any number of surnames but refers to himself as a simple, unpretentious verb?"

"The name..." Wurt sighed with brave forbearance. "...escapes me."

"Quite understandable, it's an elusive number. Poor chap only gets it right himself three tries out of ten. You say he's moved in. If that's so, I can put you onto a good thing — there's heavy betting at the Castle Castle Pub that Win Trewsbury is on the milk train to London."

Wurt considered this, aided by another absent swig of what, from the aroma, I took to be brass polish.

"Win Trewsbury." Wurt looked to the heavens, as though on the cusp of an epiphany, but then seemed to see it flutter away. "No, that couldn't be it. Said he was a Castle Carnaby, he did. Claimed his right of residence."

"Win Trewsbury is a Castle Carnaby?" I marvelled. "Even by the standards of an evening of decidedly surprising turns, this is an unanticipated anti-clockwise ring junction."

Wurt, however, was admirably stoic in the face of this front-page sensation. For some moments he focused on the darkness of the evening and together we listened to the crickets. The butler nodded at some slow, sneaking realisation and mechanically raised his flask to his lips.

"I seen him," Wurt declared, in the tone of a victory over brass polish.

"Who?" I asked. "Trewsbury?"

"In the cemetery," Wurt said in proud affirmative.

"Ah, yes, you would have," I said. "He spends rather a lot of time there, performing some sort of genealogical research, he says. Can't really recommend the place, myself — it's plenty picturesque, certainly, but accommodations are small and lacking in many modern comforts."

"The peculiar thing, though, Mister Bisjoly, is I seen him at four or maybe five o'clock one morning last week."

"In the cemetery, Wurt? What were you doing in the cemetery at four or five o'clock in the morning?"

"Sleeping, sir, in one of the crypts. I don't recall how I come to be sleeping in one of the crypts, but I woke up there with a holy thirst and a thundering headache."

"Now that is odd," I said. "Same exact thing happened to me, only this evening. What was Mister Trewsbury doing there?"

"Just talking, they were."

"They, Wurt?" I said. "Are you in a position to flesh out the pronoun?"

"That Trewsbury bloke..." said Wurt, as though stating what he thought was the obvious, "...and Mrs Ludovica."

CHAPTER FOURTEEN

No Man is Immune to the Italian Moon

I wound my way up the dimly lit stairs of the north tower to Bunty's room and rapped an amiable melody on her door. One of those happy, tappity-tap-tap-tap numbers that are widely known to be irreproducible by the forces of darkness.

From within came the subtle sound of someone suddenly ceasing to do something that was already quite idle. A pause. A series of soft footfalls. A whisper from the other side of the door.

"Speak your name, if you have one."

"Several," I replied pacifically. "But you may think of me as your dear old Anty Boisjoly. I've brought you something."

"My amulet?" Bunty still spoke softly, but now in that stage whisper that, it is widely believed, renders voice directional.

"I think so." I drew the item from my pocket and examined it. "Does it resemble a locust, stunned in the act of brushing its teeth, the moment captured forever in a pony glass of aspic?"

The door snapped open about six inches and Bunty's hand appeared.

"Gimme."

"I have two almost identical amulets, Bunty," I said, holding up both. "One must be Sid's."

Bunty peered through the crack. Behind her was mostly darkness, dappled with flickering candlelight.

"That one." She pointed at the hideous artefact on the right.

"How can you tell?" I asked. "To me they're identical and equally lovely."

"It has my aura." Bunty spoke in hushed, awed tones.

"Oh, I don't know," I said. "I find you a very handsome woman. I'm sure many would agree."

"May I please have my amulet now, Mister Boisjoly?"

"But of course," I said, although I continued to study the thing. "Curious thing — why do you suppose it is that Ludovica never got an amulet?"

"That's all Cecil's fault. He made Wandalen Kettle pay rent on the pub."

"Yes, of course, I recall now," I said. "Nevertheless, the amulets were, I believe, a separate item in the Kettle catalogue. She charges extra, as she does for the lucrative line in liquorice-on-a-string."

"Ludovica didn't want one." Bunty looked earnestly into my eyes. "I told her to get one."

"Sceptical, was she?" I asked. "Well, you tried — there's just no convincing some people of the dangers of a four hundred year old myth about witches and malignant fog."

"Oh, she knew the curse was real, she just thought that she was stronger — Ludovica was a practitioner of the dark arts."

"You're not saying that Cecil Carnaby, dedicated student of the coldly scientific school of moving dirt from one place to another, married a witch."

Bunty nodded, her wide eyes goggling in their sockets.

"How did you know?" I asked. "Did she tell you?"

"She kept it a secret," said Bunty. "But I could tell. For one thing, she was always reciting incantations in a secret, mystical language."

"Sound anything like *'Che giova nelle fata dar di cozzo?'*"

Bunty gasped and closed the door to the width of one eye.

"It's Italian," I explained. "It means, *'When choosing between riding a runaway train or standing in front of it, why not splash out on a first-class ticket?'* A somewhat liberal translation, I confess, from Dante's Inferno, on which I have recently had much cause to meditate."

"Well, she also exercised a strange power over the men of the castle," persisted Bunty.

"That, too, is Italian," I said. "I once proposed to a woman because she happened to wish me a *'buona sera'* on the shore of Lago Como during a full moon. It didn't work out, in the end — before I even learned her name, Nanny Doyle took me back to the hotel and sent me to bed. I often think of what might have been."

"She had Barnaby under her spell," confided Bunty in a low, exalted hush. "The poor, gullible gewgaw was putting on all sorts of ridiculous airs."

"Is he not always like that?"

"This was worse."

"Surely that's not possible."

"Acting like he had money and prospects, implying that he had important friends in London." Bunty's tone impugned the very idea that anyone from London could be important and/or friendly. "It's part of the spell, you understand. I'm immune, of course, so I could see the effect on Barnaby, Cecil, Wselfwulf..."

"Wselfwulf was smitten with Ludovica?"

"Every bit as much as Cecil and Barnaby." Bunty was warming to her passionate defamation of the deceased, doubtless swept away by the novel experience of someone listening to her. "With Wselfwulf it was all about how he belongs to this club of rich idlers and how he spends all his time just drinking and gambling and meddling in police business."

"Ha, you don't say," I said. "Sad what a chap will claim just to impress a girl."

"Oh, she wasn't impressed by any of that," scoffed Bunty.

"Oh, no?"

"Of course not — who would be impressed by such behaviour? Even if any of it was true."

"Even if what now?"

"I mean to say, *especially* if it was true."

"Yes, indeed, but just to focus for a tick on this thing you call 'true'," I said. "You're saying it's not?"

"Of course it's not. Wselfwulf is no more a man-about-London than I am."

"I must confess, I'm shocked."

"No you're not," said Bunty, flatly.

"No, you're right, I'm not," I said. "I'm a little surprised that you worked it out though."

"I didn't..." Bunty's eyes widened in that contagious way eyes sometimes have of widening. "...I was told by a vision of our ancestors... confirmed by the fact that he's worn the same suit for ten years, and he once severely upbraided Cressida for lighting a cigarette from the chafing dish."

"Yes, that would definitely lure the real Carnaby to the surface."

"I take it he's your valet, or some such."

"Got my number too, have you?" I observed. "These ancestral visions are certainly up-to-date on London society."

"May I have my amulet back now, Mister Boisjoly?"

Cressida's room, as directed by Bunty, was in the main house, of which until then I'd seen only the kitchen and dining room. The upper floors trended dark and close, as mediaeval manors will, with rough stone walls and gas lanterns, stocky, dark-stained hardwood doors, and a heavy ambience of woodsmoke, all combined to present a jolly dungeon aesthetic.

"Who is it?" Cressida sang from within in reply to my chirpy tapping.

I confess I was rather dreading this moment. Had to be done, of course — I needed to gauge everyone's reaction to Anty Boisjoly away from his natural habitat of a hole in the ground — but I could hardly tell Cressida that, and I was anxious how she might interpret a pretext to knock on her door late at night, in light of her weakness for my countless charms.

"Anty Boisjoly," I called, with room-service formality.

"Oh," was the muted reaction. "It's you." Difficult to interpret, but this didn't sound instantly like someone surprised nor, if it comes to it, particularly pleased to learn that Anty Boisjoly still lived.

"It is," I admitted. "I've brought your amulet."

The door swung open wide and Cressida suspended herself between handle and jamb, like a languid, luxuriantly sequined cobweb. Behind her was a room billowy with diaphanous drapery and bright with yellow lamp light.

"Here you are." I held up the remaining amulet. "The miscreant, you'll be pleased to know, will be severely punished with an extra ration of buns from the Towny-Castle Pub, and a seed cake."

"Thanks." Cressida relieved me of the hideous thing and drained it onto a table or some such surface out of sight beside the door. "I understand you think you've solved Ludovica's murder."

"Vickers told you that, did he?" I asked. "I asked him to keep it under his hat, but Vickers hasn't kept the same hat for more than a week since the Nobby Dobby went off the market in 19 nought-nought."

Cressida shook her head. "I got it from Bunty. She doesn't believe it, of course. Thinks you're Wselwulf's dimwitted dogsbody."

"I prefer to think of myself as a journeyman."

"Know what I think?"

"That sequins should be mandatory?"

"I think that it's you who's the nosy detective."

"Knowing, I think you mean," I gently corrected. "I take tremendous pains to hide my acumen. It just sort of leaks out, sometimes."

"Nobby told me." Cressida seemed as surprised by this as I was. "He says that Wselfwulf is *maître d'* at some posh hotel or something."

"Something like that," I confessed. "Keep it between us, what? Above all, don't tell Vickers."

"So, if it wasn't the curse that took Ludovica, how did we all manage to see exactly that?"

"Mainly you saw what you expected to see, and you all expected to see the same thing," I explained. "Ludovica wasn't fetched up. She wasn't even killed in a fall. She was deliberately murdered with a loose rock after willingly climbing to the bottom of the scarp."

"By whom?"

"You might have some insight into that, actually," I said. "I understand that you remained on the wall after Barnaby went to confer with Lint, Bunty, and Wurt in the courtyard."

"Who told you that?"

"Candidly, I've lost track. Approximately everyone. Didn't you?"

"I might have. Why?"

"The murder will have taken place some ten minutes later than we thought — whoever did it would have had just enough time to cross the back garden, climb down the steps, perform the crime, and possibly return to the castle, or possibly not. If you saw someone cross the back garden immediately after Ludovica was fetched up by the mists, then you probably saw the killer."

"No..." Cressida put a reflective finger to a deflective cheek. "...No, I don't think I was on the wall. I must have come downstairs after Nobby. Tell you who I did see crossing the back garden to the scarp, though — Ludovica."

"Yes, I think that was established quite early on in the investigation," I pointed out.

"I mean, practically every night since she got here — she and Uncle Cecil didn't share a room, you know — when he'd go to work on his memoir she'd nip into the back garden. Probably thought nobody saw her, but I usually have a cigarette on the wall around then."

"Is there anything especially embarrassing about being in the back garden after cocktails?" I asked. "She wasn't pretending to be Puck, was she? It's very awkward when one is caught doing that."

"Puck?"

"Mischievous sprite from *Midsummer Night's Dream*," I reminded her. "Prances about the woods at night, distributing love potion with no regard for the consequences."

"Symbolic, I assume, of listless idlers."

"Possibly you had to be there."

"I'm sure I don't know what Ludovica was up to." Cressida said this with a tone that suggested that a) Ludovica was 'up to' something and b) Cressida had a quite solid idea what it was.

"I take it she met someone on these occasions."

"You don't think I spied on her, do you?"

"I rather do think that, yes."

"Well, I didn't," claimed Cressida. "I have better things to do with my time, and it was hardly any of my business. Now, though, it seems rather pertinent that she was stealing away to meet someone other than her husband, don't you think?"

"But you can't say who it was, or even if she wasn't just going to the garden to do a spot of indiscriminate prancing."

"Who else could it be but Barnaby?"

"Barnaby Carnaby?" I asked, aghast and yet, delighted at the opportunity to recite the name.

"Who else? Wurt?" proposed Cressida without conviction. "I doubt it was Wselfwulf — he thought she was a gold-digger — and there's no one else in the castle."

"You rule out anyone from outside the castle, then."

"I do," agreed Cressida. "I think Ludovica was a gold-digger, too. Now, if you'll excuse me, Mister Boisjoly, Win is expecting me in the library for cocktails — he's promised to show me where he was bitten by an ocelot."

"You bungled that rather expertly, old man."

Barnaby had appeared in the doorway of what I took to be his room in time to hear his sister's parting words. He was dressed for dinner and the 1923 revival of *Tonight's the Night,* and he held a cocktail shaker as though he had near-term plans to shotput it.

"I fear you'll have to be more specific, Nobby," I replied. "It's been a long day."

"My sister's affections are fleeting," he explained. "She was quite enamoured with you until Win Trewsbury knocked on the door."

"Was she? How subtle women are."

"Have you met him?" asked Nobby. "Smashing chap. Do you know that he once broke a horse? Can you imagine how much strength that must take? Comes from eating rattlesnake, of all things. Snooter?" Barnaby gave the motion a sloshing obligato with the cocktail shaker.

"A very civilised proposal. Just a whisky and whisky, if you've got all the ingredients on hand."

Barnaby solemnly shook his head and vigorously shook his shaker. "I'm making us a couple of Bee's Knees. It's all anyone who matters drinks in Hollywood these days." He retreated into his room and I followed. "Prax wouldn't let me have any honey, so I'm using strawberry jam, and a little innovation of my own."

Barnaby's room was comparatively spacious and more of a suite, so that we found ourselves in a worn-leather-furnished ante-room, decorated with ageing theatre playbills and a mixology wall of liquors, liqueurs, specifics, measuring vessels and every possible form and norm of glassware.

"I'm a bit fussy about mixed cocktails, as a rule, Nobs old bean," I demurred, as he poured two even *coupes* and garnished them with nutmeg scraped directly from the stone.

"Of course you are, as am I." Barnaby handed over a glass. "As are all society gentlemen."

I took a gracious sip and was instantly won.

"That's actually quite good, Nobby." I took another, fuller trial. "Properly original, too. Gin, obviously, and there are the strawberries — local, I'd say, preserved within the year... lemon — extract but perfectly serviceable... and..." I tested another sample. "I'm usually quite good at this..." I exhaled slowly and nasally. "...it's not... alum?"

"Just a pinch. I got it from the kitchen. Prax uses it for pickling beets, I think, and Lint uses it for whitening the laundry or sharpening the knives or some such thing."

"Extraordinary."

"You like it then."

"I do."

"Not too much alum?"

"I stand in amazement as I say this but, no, not too much alum."

Barnaby beamed under the adulation. "Capital. I'm going to make one for Win. I was trying to decide between a Bee's Knees and my Gin Rickey with chicory and gooseberries."

"Happy to give that a go, if you're still undecided."

"I'd like to, Anty..." Barnaby began reloading the cocktail shaker. "...but I told Win I'd be along presently. Smashing chap, that, don't you think?"

"He's my idol," I claimed. "Do you get much of a chance to share this talent of yours?"

"Not really," sighed Barnaby. "The rest of the castle aren't much for cocktails, really, apart from Sid, and she won't drink anything that's not fizzy or pink."

"How about Ludovica?" I asked. "Were you able to tempt her?"

"One doesn't bandy a lady's name, Anty," said Barnaby with a Shakespearean show of urbane detachment. "I think you know that. Besides..." He leered conspiratorially and swirled his drink rakishly. "...she was my uncle's wife."

"I meant with respect to mixed drinks, Nobby."

"Oh, right. Uhm, no, not so very much. Ludovica was more of a red wine sort. Italian, don't you know. Do I understand correctly that you think you know who killed her?"

"I've narrowed down the list of suspects considerably — I can say with absolute certainty that Ravena Sooter had nothing to do with it. Did Sid tell you that I'd worked it out?"

"Uhm..." Barnaby sipped reflectively on his Bee's Knees. "Might have done. Can't recall."

"You two don't have a lot of secrets, do you?"

"Secrets? No, of course not. What sort of secrets?"

"I mean to say, you don't keep much from one another," I clarified.

"Oh, secrets. From each other. Quite, quite..." Barnaby posed a casual elbow on his mantelpiece.

"Talking of which, how did you come to know that cousin Wselfwulf isn't the London Boisjoly he claims to be?" I asked.

"You know how these things are, Anty. Little details, I suppose. One picks up the cues. It was quite obvious to me that Wselfwulf was, shall we say, something other than scrupulous in his accounting of his work with the police."

"Read about it in the newspaper, did you?"

"Well, in point of fact, I did, but doubtless I'd have come round to the essentials in good time." Barnaby finished his drink and poised to begin shaking up a new supply but paused to say, "I say, that doesn't need to go any further, what? No value in anyone else knowing Wselfwulf's innocent little dissimulation. He has troubles enough already."

CHAPTER FIFTEEN

Setting the Betting on an Early June Wedding

The upper residential floor of the main house resembled, unsurprisingly, the lower residential floor, with just a touch more of an air of the forbidden, owing mainly to the fact that I was sneaking about.

The hall was dark and the doors heavy and worn and oak — identical to each other and those of the floor below. Consequently, I was forced to orient by the celebrated Boisjoly nose. Ludovica, it turned out, was an *Aqua di Parma* girl, judging by the subtle scent of the fourth and final door which, unfortunately as it would soon prove, was unlocked. I went in.

It was just the sort of room one would expect a continental of taste and refinement to hew out of a stone cell, like those early American pioneers who would hack four-star hotels out of redwoods and mud and any convenient source of apex predator. A panoramic painting of a villa in the Italian style was leaning on the mantelpiece, not yet hung, next to a Chianti bottle stopped with a candle. A black lacquer and hand-painted *scrivania* creaked under papers and books beneath the window, beyond which night was a curtain of black. A tall, suspicious, built-in bookshelf was a disordered heterogeneity in Italian, French, and English, and an immense, winged, high-backed chair faced away from the room and into a reading corner, flanked by side tables and a hanging brass oil lamp.

I was drawn to the writing desk, initially, because it had papers on it. The feral and irresistible draw of someone else's handwritten documents is almost certainly what blinded me initially to the glaring truth of the situation. There were your standard lists and letters in Italian, and bureaucratic documents in English, a half-box of envelopes and a nearly empty sheaf of writing paper. I was about to take up a London county marriage registration certificate when I realised, among other important facts at hand, that all the documents were perfectly legible. If the room was empty, why was the lamp lit?

"What are you doing in my wife's room, Boisjoly?"

Cecil, who had been rather unsportingly concealed in the high-backed reading chair, drew himself to his full height.

"Oh, what ho, Cecil." I instinctively and rapidly withdrew my hand from the desk, which of course made me appear even guiltier. "Is this Ludovica's room?" I gazed about me, looking as much as possible like Vickers emerging from a reverie in new surroundings. "Very agreeable. Comfortable, yet classical. Is that an original edition of *Malombra?*"

"Why are you nosing through my wife's private effects?"

"Nosing? I'm not nosing. Why, the very idea is laughable," I said, and added "ha ha ha ha", by way of demonstrating the technique.

"Perhaps you'd like to explain, Mister Boisjoly, why I shouldn't throw you bodily out of my castle."

"Well, I suppose, setting aside the duty of the host to his guests which some, perhaps even the best of us, might describe as the foundation of the British way of life..." this was an argument which I could see, at a glance, had failed to captivate. It was vital, though, that I remain in the castle long enough to solve the murder. I smiled, probably somewhat vacantly, while I reflected on some line of reasoning that would resonate with the family patriarch.

"Honest mistake," I finally flailed. "Right room, wrong floor."

"Eh?"

"I don't wish to be indiscreet, Cecil," I said coolly, "but as you're determined to charge the walls of a thousand years of civilised convention, I was calling upon your niece, Cressida."

"Cressida?" The tack, it would appear, had taken Cecil right between the eyes. "You mean, you and Cressida…"

"I do mean Cressida and me, yes." I employed, even if it's me saying so, exactly the right measure of hauteur.

Cecil's attitude had changed rapidly from trespassed landholder to offloading inlaw, and just as quickly it changed again. His smile fell away and he said, "You know she's got no money, don't you?"

I shot each cuff in turn, and flicked a speck of dust from my sleeve. "Your familial concern is noted, Cecil, and appreciated, but I am amply provided for."

"Yes, yes, I daresay you are." Cecil assumed a solicitous, almost avuncular demeanour that he wore as naturally as I might wear mutton-chop sideburns. "You may as well know, Boisjoly, everyone else already does — these so-called Castle Carnabys won't be able to leech off the estate much longer."

"Of course," I said. "You don't want to be carrying this business of familial concern to wild extremes. But I thought all descendants of Ranulf had perpetual right of residence."

"Sure," acknowledged Cecil. "They've got the right to live here, but they don't have the right to live here comfortably."

"Speaking as a short-term resident of the castle, Cecil, they don't. If you don't mind me mentioning it, the only difference between the hot water and cold is that the hot is slightly less brown but smells marginally more of turps."

"It'll be a whole lot less comfortable when there's no water at all, nor lamp fuel, firewood, or staff."

"Indubitably," I agreed. "Are those likely contingencies?"

"I've already given the staff their notice, and cancelled all standing trade orders — the butcher, the coal merchant, everything." One could assume that while announcing these measures Cecil had been rubbing his hands together, but he

135

wasn't. He corrected that oversight now. "So you see, Boisjoly, you've come along at just the right moment for Cressida." Cecil took a break from hand rubbing and regarded me circumspectly. "You're really in love with her."

"I am to Troilus as she is to... well, Cressida," I said. "With, perhaps, a few more lines. Have you ever seen that play? It's as if the bard had written *Henry the Fifth* and titled it 'Farewell to Falstaff'."

"Shakespeare, right?"

"Clear through."

"I thought so." Cecil held his chin meditatively. "I wonder what it is that you and Cressida find to talk about."

"She's a woman of hidden depths," I claimed. "Only earlier this evening she was sharing the most penetrating insights into the significance of the character of Puck in *Midsummer Night's Dream.*"

"Are you sure we're talking about the same Cressida? The tinsel-brained clothesline?"

"Unless there's another sequinned seductress on the premises," I said. "And I will trouble you, Cecil, to not refer to the woman I love as 'tinsel-brained' assuming, of course, it is intended as a pejorative. I'm not sure she'd see it as such."

"Well, this is fine." Cecil took an unpracticed and ungifted run at a smile. "How about June?"

"Not sure I follow the train of thought but, of course, you may call her June, if she's agreeable."

"I mean a June wedding."

"Ah, well, truth to be told, Cecil, I haven't actually asked her yet," I said. "I'm working up the best approach. Hers is a personality of inscrutable mystery."

"I'll bet you don't get past 'will you...' before she's picked out names for your children."

"My understanding is that she's already operating from a very tidy shortlist."

There's no such thing as the perfect segué, of course, and frankly I wasn't fussy. I would have been prepared to simply shout 'fire!' if that's what it took to move onto the next topic, but I spotted a subtle compromise. "Lovely villa, that." I nodded at the painting on the mantelpiece. "Ludovica's?"

"Mine, now, I guess." Cecil gazed sadly at the past, then a cheerful thought came to him. "Make a lovely spot for a honeymoon. It's shuttered, at the moment, but a little local lucre would soon set that right."

"I have little talent for renovations," I confessed. "I had a fire in my Chelsea pied-à-terre last year that, quite frankly, I've only just now remembered. It's a condition, you understand. Nerve specialists refer to it as 'inertia'."

"The villa just needs airing out," encouraged Cecil, invulnerable, apparently, to a hint. "Just stay clear of the reflecting pool."

"That I might not fall in love with my own image, like Narcissus?" I asked. "Kind of you to notice. I learned many years ago to never linger long before a mirror."

"No, it's stagnant. I was never able to get it to drain properly," said Cecil. "You'd think something died in there."

In service of a thorough census of those displaying guilt or guilt-like symptoms, I sought directions to Carnaby's room, received and acted upon them.

"What ho, Wself old wulf," I hailed as Carnaby opened the door.

A cloud of Vickersian confusion passed over his face. Doubtless I was witnessing the moment all men leading double lives require to recall which one is in current employ. Something appeared to get caught in the gears, though, and the result was an unfortunate cross-breed.

"Ah, yes, what ho, Anty. Tempt you with a spot of something?" said Carnaby, getting the chummy words largely right but delivering them as though they meant 'Good evening, Mister Boisjoly, sir. Shall I prepare cocktails?'

"Just a small whisky and wibbly-water." I followed Carnaby into his room — a brown and browner leather ensuite appointed not unlike the lounge of the Juniper — and installed myself in an odeon chair. "Unless you have any strawberry jam and alum on hand."

Carnaby considered this as though from a distance, situated somewhere between castle and club.

"I fear not, sir. Possibly the kitchen could provide…"

"I wouldn't want to disturb the staff during these trying times," I said. "Is it true that Cecil is all but shutting the place down?"

Carnaby brought forth a subtly soda'd scotch. "I fear so. Staff was given notice this evening, and it has been announced that the household budget is to be drastically reduced."

"It can hardly have been a king's ransom as it was," I observed. "But I understand the objective is to drive the remaining Castle Carnabys into the snow."

"The more charitable view might be that the castle has few sources of revenue from which to draw," said Carnaby. "I myself, prior to Cecil's return, endeavoured to sell certain properties, but I was prevented by the terms of Ranulf Carnaby's bequest. Only the eldest male Castle Carnaby has executive powers."

"So I'm told. Has the castle anything worth selling, apart from the castle?"

"There remains only one property which brings no income," said Carnaby, somewhat vaguely.

"The Castle Castle Pub," I guessed.

"I proposed very generous terms to Wandalen Kettle," said Carnaby. "But she preferred the current arrangement."

"You mean the one in which she pays no rent."

"Yes. That one."

"I wonder why." I mused on the point, aided by a sip of whisky. "But in any case, that arrangement no longer holds — Wanadalen might be more disposed toward buying the pub now."

"Of course..." Carnaby absently sipped his own drink. "...as would Odd, no doubt."

"I take it the Town Castle Pub is also castle property then."

"It is," confirmed Carnaby. "I don't wish to make unkind conjecture..."

"So you'd like me to do it on your behalf," I concluded. "It's my pleasure, Carnaby, and my gift. After Cecil succeeds in scattering the Castle Carnabys to the four winds, he'll then force Odd and Wandalen to purchase their pubs and live lavishly on the proceeds."

"This is in line with my thinking, yes."

"If it's lavish living he's after — and, speaking as an enthusiast, I can endorse it almost unreservedly — can he not just live lavishly in his wife's villa?"

"The plan may have begun as an effort to impress Ludovica," said Carnaby. "I gathered from her that she believed Cecil to be extremely wealthy."

"And he's not?"

"He may have exaggerated his financial situation somewhat."

"Yes, I heard that Ludovica inspired the imagination of the men of Carnaby Castle." I swirled my drink prosecutorially at Carnaby.

He swirled his drink defensively, but without conviction.

"She was a most charming woman," admitted Carnaby. "But my overtures toward her were initially innocent and, in complete candour, calculated to draw out her true intentions."

"I think you're going to need to elaborate on that bit of choice rumminess, Carnaby."

"You see, sir, I and, I believe, others, suspected that Ludovica might have been something of an opportunist..."

139

"You believed that she was after the Carnaby riches."

"Such as they are, yes, sir."

"I know all that, Carnaby," I said. "It is not to this ripe rumminess I refer — I draw your attention specifically to your choice of the words 'initially innocent' to characterise the nature of your overtures to the lady. What became of said overtures, after they were no longer 'initial'?"

Carnaby's eyebrows raised in slow surmise. He swirled his drink but vainly, as though the act of drinks swirling was, at best, neutral. The slightest, almost imperceptible contours jittered about the corners of his mouth, threatening mischievously to become a smile. I instantly recognised the symptoms.

"You're not about to issue the Carnaby Castle classic platitude about bandying lady's names, are you?" I asked. "It's not as though there could be any confusion about who we're discussing."

"You must understand, Mister Boisjoly, she was very…"

"Italian?"

"In every respect," pleaded Carnaby. "You should have heard how she pronounced Wselfwulf."

"And was there a full moon in play?"

"On at least one occasion, yes."

"Well, I can certainly sympathise, Carnaby, me old Casanova," I said. "But I've been rather boring Inspector Wittersham with assurances of your irreproachable civility. It's been my main line of defence, in fact, whenever he toys idly in his whimsical way of arresting you for the murder of Ludovica Carnaby."

"I could never have harmed her, Mister Boisjoly," assured Carnaby with pronounced earnestness. "I believe that I loved her."

CHAPTER SIXTEEN

The Deceptive Exterior of the Future Anterior

Like most people, I recall with mixed feelings the day I put the finishing touches on the future anterior form of 'capio, capere: to capture' and knowing, as well as I knew my own name, that I had finished Latin. I could cite every tense of every group, and I knew their respective principal parts, backwards and forwards and to the rhythm of the metronome that our second-form master had added to his teaching arsenal, it was rumoured, during his time as a prisoner of the Chinese during the Opium Wars.

So, I'd made it out the other side of Latin and reckoned we'd spend the next five years translating Cicero. This suited me fine. I liked Cicero — he had an accommodating way of writing to his mate, Atticus, about daily life in Rome as though he fully expected his letters to be one day read by second-form boys who needed to know exactly where and when to be if they were going to play a pivotal role in the assassination of Julius Caesar.

Then, the very next day, Mister Skittlewit (our Latin master was in fact an acutely clever man, but his real name was Middlewick and so, obviously, our hands were tied) told us to open our books to chapter eleven, 'The Passive Voice' and, in a stroke, my net understanding of Latin decreased by half, plus the past participle.

Carnaby's revelation was like that of Mister Skittlewit — I knew less about the murder of Ludovica Carnaby than I did before I spoke to him.

With the exception of Wurt, who was doubtless above that sort of thing, every man in the castle had so far claimed the affections of Ludovica. I hastened, then, to the library, to see if Win would voluntarily complete the collection.

I dispensed with the traditional 'What ho' as I slipped into the library, because Cressida was performing the previously thought scientifically impossible task of accompanying herself on the harpsichord to *Sweet Georgia Brown* and — this is the impossible bit — making it somehow work. Her left hand made of the instrument a brass quartet, her right a rhythm section, and her voice had that close-to-the-road rasp that requires no less than twenty Woodbines a day to stay in form.

Nobby struck a metropolitan manner by the mantle, and Win ranged himself on the divan, a Bee's Knees *à la Barnaby* in one hand and a great flaming sausage of a cigar in the other.

Before the applause died away, Sid cranked the ancient keyboard up to the speed of swing and sizzled through *Varsity Drag,* slowing only marginally to give the harpsichord what very convincingly sounded like a banjo solo.

"Takes me back." Win nodded his approval and bit a mouthful of smoke off his cigar. "You sound just like those shantooze I used to hear in the speakeasies in Chicago, when I was running rum from Canada."

"Another sploosh of juice?" Nobby shook the cocktail shaker and Win held out his glass for a top-up. "You were a bootlegger, Win?" marvelled Nobby. "Tell us, what's Al Capone like?"

"Never met the man."

"Oh." This frank admission seemed to hit Barnaby hard, and he looked briefly baffled by it.

"Any Bee's Bits left over, Nobs?" I asked.

"Afraid not, Anty." As he said this Barnaby drained the cocktail shaker into his glass. "Unless you want me to make more, Win?"

"I'm alright," said Win. Cressida snuggled onto the divan next to him and mingled her cigarette smoke with that of his cigar.

"You're settling in well, Win," I observed. "Inspector Wittersham told me that you'd probably shied for the sunny shores of London."

"Was it you put that policeman onto me?"

"Not directly, no," I said. "But I played a pivotal role."

"Seems to me some people should just mind their own business."

"Not really my strong suit," I confessed. "And you rather invited scrutiny by introducing yourself to my man as John Jacob Jingleheimer Schmidt or some variation thereof, and following that up with a steady stream of unfiltered twaddle about horse-bothering and loitering on mountaintops."

"Why should I tell you my real name?" Win expressed a cloud of smoke from his nose. "And the rest is all true. Why would anyone lie about climbing mountains?"

"To impress Vickers, I assumed. He's an imposing personality."

"You've climbed mountains?" gushed Sid. "What was the highest? Or the most dangerous?"

"No real danger in climbing a mountain, if you know what you're doing," claimed Win.

"One simply wears a parachute, Sid," said Barnaby, dismissively. "Isn't that right, Win?"

"A parachute? To climb a mountain? Of course not. What good would a parachute be if you fell off a mountain?" scoffed Win. "Tell you when a parachute did save my life, though, if you want to hear it..."

"Oh, yes, tell us, Win," swooned Sid.

"This is about five years ago..." Win drew recollectively on his cigar. "For reasons best left to conjecture, I had to get from Southern Rhodesia to Cairo, and I talked my way onto a little monoplane that happened to be going that way."

"Rather a long flight for a little plane, isn't it?" I asked.

"Well, exactly." Win adopted my motion with a stab of his smoke bomb. "We're barely in the air an hour and the pilot says he's putting in at Lilwonge which was, at the time, nothing but a garrison. For other reasons best left to conjecture, that didn't suit my plans, and so I bailed out over Harare. Landed neatly on the shore of the Manyame. Good thing it wasn't rainy season, or I'd still be there."

"Was this the occasion for which you received your Caterpillar Club pin?" I asked.

"Know about that too, do you?"

"I was under the impression that membership was awarded to those who were forced to jump from disabled aircraft."

"And so it is," confirmed Win. "The plane went down in the jungle in a ball of flame. Pilot barely made it out."

"However did you know?" marvelled Sid.

"I didn't, in point of fact." Win discharged three perfectly formed smoke rings in succession toward the ceiling. "I put my cigar in a box of mail before decamping. Pure chance it set the plane on fire."

"Yes," I agreed. "What an extraordinary coincidence."

"You've been everywhere," gushed Sid.

"Most rewarding, travel, I've always felt," added Nobby. "Ever been to Eastbourne?"

"Uh, no, I don't think so," said Win.

"Whatever brings you to Hoy, of all places?" asked Nobby.

"Well, if you must know, I came to meet Ludovica."

"You'd never met your stepmother before coming to Hoy?" I asked.

"Stepmother?" Sid put a small but meaningful amount of divan between her and Win. "Ludovica was your stepmother?"

"Win's father was her previous husband," I explained. "Weren't you invited to the wedding, Win?"

"The old man and I were rather on the outs, at that point." Win examined his cigar from beneath hooded eyes. "Hadn't seen each

144

other in a few years. I didn't even know he was dead until I saw the announcement of Ludovica's marriage to Cecil in the Times."

"Poor Win." Sid put a hand on his. "What happened?"

"Oh, just the usual father and son gnashing of teeth and clashing beliefs, don't you know?" Win spoke vaguely from within a cloud of smoke. "Also, it was his plane I set on fire over Harare. Cost him the entire African postal concession."

"Oh, dear."

"Hmm. Had to pay pretty hefty damages, too."

"Hang on." Cressida withdrew her hand and returned to the business at hand. "I thought you said you were a Castle Carnaby."

"And so I am," insisted Win. "Your uncle Cecil is married to my stepmother. That makes him my stepfather, making me a Castle Carnaby."

"That's not how it works," pointed out Cressida.

"Who is the law or even convention to define that most hallowed and hospitable of words, 'family'?" I asked. "I have a half-uncle by marriage who, in a non-binding civil ceremony, retroactively adopted a poor little orphan boy, name of Edward the VI. Never a word of complaint from either of them. She's right, though, Win. That's not how it works."

"Of course it is," persisted Win. "She married my father, didn't she? That makes her my mother. She killed my father, married Cecil, he's my father. Simple."

"Just a second." Cressida withdrew from the divan altogether, ostensibly to crush out her cigarette in a saucer on the harpsichord. "Ludovica killed your father?"

"This is Win's pet theory," I explained. "The man is missing."

"You ever meet my father, Boisjoly?" asked Win, almost certainly, rhetorically.

"To my lasting regret, no."

"He's not the sort to go missing, trust me." Win spat a scornful of smoke from the side of his mouth. "He's dead, and she killed him."

"Why did you come to Hoy, again?" asked Cressida.

"Just told you — I wanted to talk to Ludovica."

"And... did you...?" asked Cressida.

Before Win could answer, the door swung abruptly open and Wurt followed it swiftly into the room, having forgotten to release the handle.

"Inspector Wittersham." Wurt stood aside, swaying in gentle anticipation. After a mercifully brief but awkward pause, he retraced his steps into the hall, returned, and said, "I believe that the inspector is somewhere without... I shall endeavour to recover him." And off he went to do, possibly, exactly that.

"Right, that's me off," said Win. "I expect the inspector's thought up another dozen ways to ask the same question."

"Right-ho, Win. I'll just whip a batch of Betty Balfours, if I can scare up an ounce or two of treacle..." Barnaby spoke in descending obsequiousness, until Win was gone. He then turned to the runner up. "So, feel free to pop round, Anty, if or when you're done with the inspector." And then Barnaby, too, departed.

"Guess I'll be going too." Sid watched after the men with fists on her hips and misgivings on her lips. Then she regarded me with that old, familiar, predatory appraisal that I'd missed so very much. She took the liberty of straightening my tie against its will. "What a bore some men are, don't you find? With their mountain-climbing and parachute-jumping... such a waste of... resources."

Cressida drew herself away, tracking her nails across my lapel as she went.

Some minutes later Wurt returned and again announced, "Inspector Wittersham and Constable Blewit," but then surveyed the room slowly and realised that only I remained. "Ah," he somehow slurred. "The inspector and the constable are here, Mister Boisjoly."

"So they are," I confirmed as Blewit followed Ivor into the room. "You couldn't sort us a well-deserved bottle of brown bounty, could you, Wurt? Or something that rhymes with sport? Or splotch? Anything but Amontillado. really."

Wurt smiled distantly.

"He means drinks, Wurt," translated Ivor.

"Very good, sir." Wurt shimmied out the door.

"What ho, secular arm. What drags you out of your warm beer at this lengthening hour?"

"Wurt does," said Ivor. "He said you sent him to fetch us."

"Ah, I suppose I did, but not with any serious intent," I confessed. "I told him that you'd be interested to know that Win Trewsbury was on the premises."

"Is he?"

"The delicate perfume of scorched tar that still lingers is that of his very cigar."

"Good to know, I suppose," said Ivor, distractedly. "I don't know that it changes anything, though. Or does it?"

"There have been developments, but their significance may be subject to debate," I said. "How strict are your views on unconventional cocktail mixes?"

"Indifferent. Why?"

"Set that aside, then. There's this, though — Win believes himself to be a Castle Carnaby, and entitled to a share of the family oofus. Cressida, distressingly, has realised the opposite — that Win is a penniless adventurer whose father died angry. This is especially worrying to any moneyed young bachelors on the premises."

"Why, particularly?"

"Because the fuse has been lit on the days of lavish living at Carnaby Castle," I explained. "Cecil has cancelled all the contracts for extravagances like heat and light, and given the staff notice of the noose."

"Given... notice?" This unsteady exclamation came from the door, at which Wurt had appeared with a jolly trolly of inspiration. He had about him a persecuted, betrayed air, as though pink elephants upon whose gentle society he once relied had proven themselves faithless friends. "Is this so, Mister Boisjoly?"

"I can only repeat what I've been told, Wurt," I said from the back foot. "I understood that you'd been told the same."

"Not to my recollection." Wurt spoke with more certitude than one would expect him to employ when speculating on his recollection. "I gather Mister Cecil plans to close the castle."

"Best discussed with him, I think, Wurt. I'd probably put my foot in it. The other foot, I suppose I should say at this stage."

"And what's to become of Mrs Stokely? Did he even think of her?" Wurt unstacked glasses and uncorked a clay whisky jug. "She's no more able to survive beyond these walls than a worm in whisky." He poured a dangerously tall one, put down the bottle with meaning, and drained the glass. "Do you one, sir?"

"Just a small one," I said. "Inspector? Constable?"

Wurt did the honours, including another quick restorative for himself, and said, "I'll be off then, unless you'll be wanting nothing else..." and without awaiting a reply for which, I confess, I'd have struggled, he weaved away.

"I think that sums up the situation to a nicety." I raised my glass in a toast to raising my glass. "Now, as for Ludovica's love affairs..."

"What?" blurted Blewit, struggling for his notepad. "You mean here? At the castle?"

"Not strictly, no. The grounds and possibly the town feature prominently in the intrigues, but I'm not convinced the geography is particularly relevant."

"More to the point, Mister Boisjoly." If the inspector has a flaw, it's a lack of appreciation for colour commentary. "With whom do you believe Ludovica Carnaby was having an affair?"

"Honestly? No one," I said. "But there are any number within these castle walls who'll happily say otherwise. Cressida, for instance, is sure that Ludovica was slipping out at night to meet up with someone, but she's not sure who. Mrs Stokely, meanwhile, is quite certain that it was everyone."

"What do the defendants have to say?"

"Barnaby is very happy to have it widely understood that he would never admit to a discreet, hot-blooded *affare appassionato* with the worldly and alluring Ludovica," I reported. "Win, of course, insists that his relationship with the late Mrs Carnaby was one of gentle animosity, while Wselfwulf, naturally, practised the stewardly art of courtly love — devoted, deep, and distant."

Ivor had been lighting a pensive pipe during my dispatch, and now he squinted through the cloud at Blewit.

"Was there anything among the effects of the deceased to indicate an affair and, if so, with whom?"

"Not a thing." Blewit answered with a firm, country confidence that it wounded me to have to contradict.

"Perhaps not as such, Constable," I proceeded nevertheless, "but there is something of note suggestive of a mysterious third party."

"Well?" puffed Ivor.

"It's not a specific thing, really. Best seen first hand." I led by example and swallowed my drink whole. "If you'll accompany me to the lady's boudoir."

The second-floor hall remained dark but a glimmer of light leaked aqueously from the bottom of Ludovica's bedroom door.

"Cecil," I explained to Ivor and Blewit. "He won't mind. He seems to appreciate my company."

I knocked on the door. "What ho, Cecil. You'll pardon the hour, but I told Inspector Wittersham about your proposal for a June wedding and he absolutely insists on coordinating cummerbunds."

This was met with the sounds of shuffling and shifting, which was to be expected, and then something which was slightly less expected; "Help... murd...DER!"

This was followed by the customary strangled cry and then the thump of a heavy body falling to a stone floor.

CHAPTER SEVENTEEN

Seek No Further a Passage to Murder

The door, of course, was locked. "Get this open, Constable." Ivor thinks quickly and had already determined that Blewit's bulkhead build was best suited to the task.

"It's a solid block of oak, Inspector," I pointed out. "You'd have as much luck trying to break down the wall."

"Who has a key?"

"Lint, certainly."

"Keep trying, Constable," instructed Ivor. "We'll split up and find the maid."

In that instance, I noticed that the next door — by process of elimination that of Cecil's room — was open.

"I have a better way, Inspector." I led him into Cecil's simple chamber. "The hidden passage — it must lead directly to Ludovica's room."

"Right — get it open and then go fetch the maid."

"Yes, of course... it's just..." I examined the fireplace, the cavity of which was clean, unbroken tile. "Not really familiar with this model. It may take me a moment."

Ivor made a sound that might have been 'gah' but, even if it wasn't, this captures the sentiment well. He vanished into the hall and I returned to my fireplace enquiries.

I quickly and scientifically determined that randomly pressing tiles and rapping on the mantel was ineffective, and then I recalled that the entrance to the passage in the library wasn't in the fireplace at all. I surveyed the room, which was an uncomplicated exercise because it was a large, stark, stone cell, containing exactly one bed, one chair, one empty desk, a sea chest, and a wardrobe, the door of which was open. Unsurprisingly on reflection, the suits and trousers had been pushed aside like a tweed and worsted curtain, revealing that the back of the wardrobe also had a door, and it opened onto a hidden passage. I plucked an oil lamp from the wall and plunged into the darkness.

The thing about hidden passages in ancient castles — and I shall likely dedicate an entire chapter to this feature when I write my acclaimed book on the subject — is that they're unpredictable. Their principal *raison d'être* is to be hidden, with the passage aspect trailing a distant second. I had expected this passage to follow the contours of the wall and lead, if not directly, at least foreseeably to the adjacent room. Instead, the path took a sharp turn down crumbling stone stairs and into, I believe, the exterior wall of the castle. Here the passage took the form of a high, narrow corridor with, on one side, stairs carved into the wall, leading back up to, presumably, other fireplaces and wardrobes and bookshelves. The other side was solid castle. Above was darkness and below was a yawning great chasm, a hundred feet above an underground watercourse and stalagmites as sharp as bayonets. The river rushed and the wind wailed like haunted souls who, unsatisfied with a choral role, also manifested as whirling and whistling bats. It was a nightmare of stone and iron and wood and rope in three-dimensional space, like the rigging of a phantom ship above a demon sea.

The worn steps led to more worn ledges, corresponding to the first and second floors of the main house, but here and there they had fallen away entirely, isolating this little island of secret passage from the greater network. The cracked and crumbling ledges, from where I stood, accessed only a handful of rooms. I ascended with intrepid dread toward where I hoped and feared Cecil lay dying.

It was about the moment — to the instant, in fact — that the wind blew out my lamp that I realised that I may well have been sharing this corridor with a murderer. The moment caught me already in a state of, let us say, apprehension, and with lightning reflexes I shut my eyes. When I opened them again a pale blue hue was seeping in through cracks between the exterior stone. I enjoyed a brief but lingering moment of fatalistic beauty. Then my heart stopped.

The nearest door burst open with an explosion of interior light and a monstrous silhouette skidded out onto the ledge in front of me. He appeared to look this way and then that and I surmised that he was briefly blinded by the change in light, and so it was probably unfortunate in hindsight that I yelped like a Cairn Terrier experiencing its first Christmas cracker.

The monstrous shadow locked on my location and instantly charged.

I flattened against the wall and, involuntarily exercising a footballing reflex that had apparently stayed with me for years, put out my foot. The amorphous juggernaut went nebulous head over formless teakettle and uttered an "oof" in the way only a tumbling constable can. He turned on his heel, our eyes met, and then he stepped back into the void.

And there he posed, hinged on his heel and suspended by his billy club, attached to Blewit's wrist by a thin leather strap, to me by the business end, and to the ropey bannister by my other hand.

"What ho, Constable." I spoke reassuringly, for Blewit had turned his head just enough to take a measure of the gravity of his situation. "Won't you join me on the terrace? Lovely view."

Blewit nodded slowly but with a certain wide-eyed urgency. I drew him perpendicular. He hugged the wall like he was reconciling with it after a long and bitter estrangement.

"What are you two playing at?" The light from the inspector's oil lamp should probably have shown him that we were playing at staying alive.

"It's Mister Boisjoly, sir," answered Blewit, still face-to-face with the wall. "The killer must have got away."

"Killer?" I repeated. "Cecil is no more?"

"Letter opener. Back of the neck."

"Telling," I observed.

"Indeed," agreed Ivor. "Did you see where he went?"

"Who?"

"The killer."

"I didn't see anyone. Did you?"

"No one here."

"Then why do you say 'he'?"

"Very well, Boisjoly, did you see anyone?"

"I was late," I said. "The hidden passage from Cecil's room was a series of doors within doors, one more cunning than the next."

Ivor surveyed the narrow deeps and alternating levels and adjudged them, succinctly, "Blimey."

"It's not as hopeless as it looks," I alleged. "There are two rooms accessible on this floor..." I referred with a nod to the dead-end ledge that lay beyond Ivor. "...and another two on the floor below. The killer couldn't have come out of Cecil's room, obviously, and is escaping as we speak from one of the other three rooms."

"Right." Ivor assumed a wobbly military bearing. "Constable, check the first floor, I'll see to this floor." And so he did.

"Very good, sir," said Blewit to his wall. He spoke absently, though, as if distracted by some higher truth.

"Why don't you mind things here, Constable," I offered. "See no one gets past you."

"Right oh, Inspector."

The lower ledge was sounder and even in the subdued light it appeared, perhaps not maintained, as such, but in regular employ. There were lamps, unlit, on the walls, and some fishing tackle leaning sportily against a sturdy chain bannister. As above, the route was short and led to a cul de sac where the stone had crumbled into the void. Two doors were accessible.

It was the first door that intrigued and worried me with its squat, menacing attitude, like a coal chute that felt it had been born for better things. More sinister still, a fitful flicker of furtive candlelight filtered through a rune carved into the door.

I steeled my nerve with a firm grip on Constable Blewit's billy club, assumed a squat, rugby stance, and pushed through.

Happily, I had little in the way of solid expectations, but I was nevertheless surprised to be met with a long, piercing, frankly impressively penetrating scream.

"Oh, what ho, Bunty." I greeted Bunty, first, in a vain effort to lower the volume, followed by, "Miss Kettle."

"Is it a demon?" asked Bunty, who was covering her eyes with both hands. She and Wandalen were opposite sides of what looked like a card table wearing an old shawl. The room was patchily lit with fat, mollified candles and decorated — if decorated is the right word, which it isn't — with bells, star charts, geometrically woven twigs and feathers, a taxidermied raven (by which I was offended on Buns' behalf) and an eclectic and eccentric clutter of trinkets and charms and talismans including, in the centre of the table, Bunty's ugly amulet, alongside what looked like an ante of civilised jewellery.

"It's Mister Boisjoly," answered Wandalen, wearily. "How can we help you, Mister Boisjoly?"

Bunty lowered her hands from her eyes. "Should we start over?"

"It won't be necessary," soothed Wandalen. "I'm sure Mister Boisjoly has more important matters to which to attend. Don't you, Mister Boisjoly?"

"Almost certainly," I agreed. "Quick question, first — has anyone else passed through here in the past four or five minutes?"

"No."

"And how long have you been here?"

"We only just started." Bunty expressed this as some sort of complaint directed, subtly but masterfully, at me.

"Well, I'll leave you to... it." I backed out the door. "You might want to keep this locked, for the foreseeable."

The second door was appreciably more door-like in appearance. Just a normal door, really, as one might find leads to a linen closet. I opened it and found it led to a linen closet.

In the same instant, Lint found the same thing. It was like looking into a dusty mirror, as I opened the passage door just as Lint opened the hall door and we reflected each other's astonishment. Between us, her head swivelling like a Brighton weather vane, was Prax.

"Evening, ladies," I said. "You haven't seen a crazed, violent lunatic in the close past, have you?"

Both women looked at me and, with emphasis, my billy club, and each said some variation of "Possibly."

I, too, looked at the billy club. "Constable Blewit loaned it to me. He has no current call for it." I slid the device into my inside flask pocket. "So, no one came through here, either?"

"Who were you expecting, Mister Boisjoly?" asked Prax.

"Would that make a difference?"

"No one has come through that door in the time we've been here."

"How long would that be, then?"

"About five minutes," speculated Prax. "Although Lint went to see what the inspector wanted. What did he want, Lint?"

"The key to Ludovica's room," answered Lint.

"What's happened?" Prax asked me.

"I'm afraid there's been another murder," I replied. "Cecil's been stabbed."

"What?" boomed a baritone from beyond Lint. She stepped aside to reveal Win at his door, outside which stood Barnaby, with a shaker of cocktails. "You mean to say that my father has been killed? Again?"

CHAPTER EIGHTEEN

Bones, Stones, and Crones What Moans Alone in the Catacombs

There's always a general fuss and flutter whenever a murder is announced, in my disturbingly broad experience of the field, and there's little value in quoting or characterising the ensuing hubbub.

Skipping over that bit, then, we arrive at a collection of Carnabys convened at the end of the first-floor hall. Bunty and Wandalen joined us from, let us call it, the scary room. Cressida poked her head out of her room. Wurt weaved up the hall from the stairs. Barnaby, Win, Lint, Prax and I, as previously inventoried, were already present.

Ivor and Blewit joined, Carnaby between them, and the entire surviving population of the castle was crowded around, hueing and crying some variation of 'What happened?' and 'Are any of us safe?' and 'Why does the constable stare in that odd manner?'

The inspector soon threw his cold water pragmatism on the festivities and sent us all to bed, further imposing an ad hoc honour system requiring us to remain there while he and Blewit secured the scene of the crime and dealt with the grim formalities. We were all invited to keep solidly schtum and I was further invited to leave the castle altogether, and so I resumed my lodgings at the Castle Pub, which brings us to breakfast.

"What ho, old heirloom." I hailed as I entered Vickers' line of vision, which had been focused on some point between Hoy and the Andromeda Nebula, from the gunfighter's post at the back of the Castle Pub. Vickers struggled to rise, or at any rate made a good show of it, and then melted back into the upholstery.

"I'm very gratified to see you again, sir."

"Likewise, Vickers," I replied, "with the slightest snick of sad news — we're extending our stay in Hoy another few days."

"Very good, sir." Vickers' gaze was a vacant vessel.

"This is Hoy, Vickers," I said.

"Yes, sir, I was just wondering…"

"Three days, so far," I said. "Unquantifiably extended. There's been another murder."

"Surely not Carnaby, the Juniper steward," fretted Vickers, loyally.

"No, this time it's Cecil Carnaby who's been sent *ad patre*. It's a sorry second best for our man Wselfwulf, though — Inspector Wittersham is probably more convinced than ever that stewarding is a nugatory sideline to his principal occupation of sequential murder."

"A theory, I take it, to which you do not subscribe."

"I do not. The man has surprising depths, though. He's been passing himself off at the castle as, with little customisation, me."

"A perfectly understandable aspiration," said Vickers, more or less reflexively.

"Well, of course, the point is, though, he's entirely failed to carry it off — everyone in the place knows that he's in service in London."

"Hardly a shameful situation, from my perspective," sniffed Vickers.

"Nor mine." I paused, then, to say, "Cheers, Odd," for the innkeeper had finally arrived with a steaming pot of brewed morning. "Indeed, if anything, Carnaby's been caught out because of his excellence in his field. Cecil Carnaby, for instance, saw his name on a letter of recommendation for a parlour maid. Incidentally, Vickers, should you outlive me, feel free to make use of Carnaby as a reference — his word could place Wurt at Buckingham Palace."

"I'll bear it in mind, sir."

"Then my soul is at rest," I said. "In any case, the point is that Carnaby is ill-suited to dissemblance. He lacks the inventive spark so vital to the subterfuge that is among the core skills of the modern murderer. One could almost say, in fact..." I trailed off, here, and likely assumed the look of stupefaction that Boisjolys in centuries past employed to avoid military service.

"Sir?"

"Ehm. Just had a rather thunderous thought, Vickers," I mused. "I can't help noticing a theme forming. Returning to Carnaby, for a moment... Yes, Odd?" I again interrupted myself for Odd had replaced the teapot, unnecessarily, and lingered in place, like something hanging from a hook backstage at a marionette theatre.

"Sir?" said Odd, as though just then noticing me.

"Was there something else?"

"Something else?" said Odd, turning the phrase over, as if encountering it for the first time. "No, no, no... yes. Actually, Mister Boisjoly, if I could have a moment of your time, in private... no offence, Mister Vickers."

"Not at all, Odd," I said. "Vickers, I shall confer with the landlord at the bar. In my absence, please transport as much of the buffet as you can carry to this table, in two roughly equal portions."

Odd ducked back behind the bar and I leaned on the counter, creating a zone of confidence.

"Tell me all, Odd, omitting no detail, no matter how embarrassing. Have you a rash you'd like to show me?"

"It's like this, Mister Boisjoly..." Odd bent beneath the hanging, overhead glassware. "It's about... London."

"London?"

"I understand you're what's known as a man-about-town in London."

"I've been less accurately described," I agreed. "How can my man-about-townity be of use to you?"

"It's a delicate situation, Mister Boisjoly."

"Have no concerns, Odd," I assured him. "London is a delicate town, populated to a man by tender hearts, full to bursting with the fellowship of man and an appreciation for spiritual poetry."

"Do you know of a bank called Aspinall's?" asked Odd in a low voice. "In Bond Street."

"No," I said, in an equally low voice. "Because it's not a bank. Aspinall's of Bond Street is a jeweller's. A very fine jeweller's, in fact."

"A jeweller's?"

"A very fine one, yes," I confirmed. "Have I been helpful?"

"There's no bank in London called Aspinall's?"

"Could be," I allowed. "It's unlikely, though. People would always be going up to the tellers and asking to have rubies reset and rings resized. In any case, the Aspinall's in Bond Street is a jeweller's."

"I see." Odd's dour face brightened at this revelation. "This is..." Once again a cloud passed over his starboard brow. "Actually, I don't see how this changes things."

"No," I commiserated. "Neither do I."

"It's like this, Mister Boisjoly..." Odd once again reduced the volume, although the population of the bar room remained precisely one barman, a valet, and a Boisjoly, and the valet was entirely occupied with cheddar. "...on the instructions of Mister Cecil, I've been paying the rent on the Castle to what I thought was a bank in London."

"Which now turns out to be a jeweller's."

"Just so. And now that Cecil is, uh, no longer in a position to, uhm..."

"Breathe?" I suggested. "How do you come to know this already, Odd?"

"People talk," said Odd, absently. "The question is, what do I do about Aspinall's?"

"Cease paying, would be my advice, Odd," I said. "Clearly Cecil found a clever way to pay his debts from the castle coffers. I take it he offered some small consideration in exchange for your discreet cooperation."

"A month rent holiday at Christmas."

"Very generous. However else poor Cecil might be remembered, at least we know that he was charitable with other people's money. Out of curiosity, how does a Hoy pub landlord pay rent to a Bond Street jeweller's?"

"Instructions to my bank," said Odd.

"You'll want to send them new instructions," I suggested. "But don't tell them that came from me — if Aspinall's ever called in my book I'd probably have to sell an arm. One of my good ones."

"Yes…" Odd considered this and what appeared to be its weighty consequences. "You don't know if the inspector is letting anyone leave the castle, do you?"

"You know, even for a barkeep, you're awfully well-informed."

"It's just… it's Wurt handles the post, whenever there's any needs taking to Chesterfield," continued Odd, as though that explained something. "We don't like to upset him. He has an affliction, you know."

"I do, the poor, brave lad. Did you help him indulge it last night, by the way?"

"I didn't see Wurt yesterday."

"At all?" I asked. "I was led to understand that he came to town last night to fetch Wandalen Kettle. I would have assumed that he'd have seized upon the opportunity to pop in here for a quick symptom and soda."

"Didn't see him."

"He must have done his drinking at, ehm, another pub, the name of which isn't Castle."

"There's only one Castle Pub in Hoy, if you're a towny," insisted Odd.

"And another if you're not," I calculated. "Nothing steadies trade like rank tribalism. I can tell you with purest certainty that Wheatsheaf-Bale Pale Ale and Ambermont Blonde — very popular in London pubs — are the same beer from the same brewery, with only subtly different labels. And yet I've seen lifelong friendships brought to a sudden and permanent end over loyalty to one brand or the other."

"I wouldn't know about that."

"I expect Miss Kettle would," I speculated. "Bit of the Barnum about her, I think. Any idea what it is she gets up to in the graveyard at night?"

"I keep well clear of Wandalen Kettle, Mister Boisjoly, and I advise you to do the same."

"Yes, so you mentioned on our first encounter," I recalled. "And I'm happy to report that, true to my word, I ignored your advice. Any inkling what business she might have in the catacombs?"

"The catacombs?" Odd spoke this with a tone that suggested that, if there were catacombs in the vicinity, it was news to him. "No, not at all. Nothing. I mean, nothing comes to mind."

"Small word of advice, Odd, that comes from my years of experience of the discipline — fibbing is very much like faking a Scottish accent when giving a policeman a false identity — the key is understatement. So many chaps get caught out rolling their Rs like an Italian tenor and peppering their explanation for being trouserless in Trafalgar Square fountain with plenty of 'Och aye!'"

Odd glanced uncomfortably around the still mainly empty bar room, and then leaned once again into the confidentiality zone.

"Rumour has it, Mister Boisjoly…" this struck me as a very good start, "…Wandalen Kettle consults with Ravena Sooter in the catacombs."

"I say, really?" I said. "What's Ravena Sooter doing in the catacombs?"

"You know about the curse, and how Ravena Sooter come to place it on the heads of the Castle Carnabys," presumed Odd.

"I do," I confirmed. "I understand that, in keeping with the latest thinking in penal science at the time, she was chucked off the scarp."

Odd nodded. "Well, the story didn't end there. Custom at the time, of course, was to burn any witches, to discourage them from coming back to life and avenging themselves."

"Sound precaution."

"But, before they could get to the body, a mist rose from the river, completely obscuring the bottom of the scarp."

"Of course. And then, when they finally descended to the river bed, the body was gone."

"Heard it already, have you?" asked Odd.

"No, not specifically, but four hundred year old myths tend to stick to the same rough developmental pattern," I explained. "Then what happened?"

"Story goes, the local coven kept the body in a secret crypt and then, generations later, mixed her bones with those of the Carnaby ancestors, in the catacombs."

"I see," I said. "To what end? Some sort of poetic revenge?"

"Nothing poetic about it, Mister Boisjoly. Ravena Sooter is in the catacombs, where she torments Castle Carnaby ancestors for all eternity."

The sky was the colourless tone of castle stone and so followed the town and countryside beyond. A cold, drizzly, half-hearted rain sprayed its ambivalence in my face as I wandered the street and lane of Hoy, giving the forces of law and order and body disposal the time to practise their art.

The cemetery lane was deserted and slick and reflective, and the fog and damp absorbed all sound, but for the ominous awk of the raven messenger of the dark.

"What ho, Buns."

The crow was perched once again on the spindly iron arch over the cemetery gate. He focused an eye of paternal reproach upon me, mimicking that air of avuncular concern I get from Vickers when he finds me asleep in the Hawthorn Hedge. I withdrew the rolled oat cake I'd reserved from breakfast in anticipation of this encounter and set it on the stone fence. Buns fluttered down to it, examined it, and then issued me a stern "Caw", as though to say 'This is all very good, but life isn't and can't be all rolled oat cakes.' Then he took up the cake in his beak and flew to the top of a mausoleum to enjoy his breakfast.

"You would do well to heed the warnings of the crow."

This sage counsel came to me, of course, from Wandalen the witch. She had ridden the wind or some such thing to sidle up to me before speaking, giving me a stuttering start.

"Preaching to the choir, Miss Kettle," I assured her. "I always listen to the crow. And the chaffinch, of course. Can't tell you how many times London wildlife have put me onto a good thing at the track. Has Inspector Wittersham already finished with the hot lights and rubber hoses?"

"The inspector sent me home last night."

"Oh, right," I said. "I thought it was only me he trusted to leave the castle."

"I was directed to remain within Hoy."

"Well, that's more like it. He told me I was welcome to go all the way back to London, if I liked. Suggested I do, in fact. He's very generous with his faith, is our Inspector Wittersham."

"He suggested that we return this evening."

"Excellent. In the meantime, I have unfinished business with those catacombs," I claimed.

"Oh, yes? Do you require a guide?"

"Know your way around the catacombs, do you?"

"The corridors of the house of the underworld keep no secrets from me."

"I have a mate like that in London. Can stand on just about any street corner and tell you merely by the rumble the time and destination of the nearest tube. Sadly, that's his only talent and very nearly his entire conversation."

During this spiritual thrust and parry, Buns had apparently finished his bun, and he announced this sombre occasion with a plaintive "Caw."

"I encourage you to take the crow's warning seriously, Mister Boisjoly." Wandalen folded her arms into her drapery and looked knowingly toward the horizon.

"I would do," I said. "But I'm having difficulty interpreting this particular prophecy. Would you have said that was a 'caw!' or more of a 'caaaaw'?"

"The crow's meaning is clear, to me. The curse is yet unsatiated, and 'ere long it will claim another."

CHAPTER NINETEEN

A Better Belter Belstead

In anticipation of dinner at the castle, I had a gourmand's supper at the pub before setting out.

The weather had expanded on its earlier theme and was now a darker shade of drab. The sun was nearing the horizon, pinched between a carpet of gloomy effluvium on the ground and full, purple clouds above. The effect was to squeeze the setting sun into a suspicious squint, scrutinising the castle with dark apprehension.

The rain was still just a consistent mist that came from all directions at once, but in the distance haze and horizon had met in a single, swirling, bloated bladder and aimed itself directly at Hoy. It rolled rapidly across the Peak District, saturating the fields and spitting lightning and grumbling great rumbles of thunder. I made it to the castle doors just in time.

"Good evening, Mister Boisjoly," pronounced Wurt with an ominous clarity.

"Evening, Wurt," I said, stepping into the cold, damp, relative comfort of the gatehouse. "Is all well? You have an unfamiliar bearing about you, if you don't mind my commenting."

"Kind of you to notice, sir," moaned Wurt. "I fear my affliction has taken a calamitous turn, and I'm no longer equal to it."

"Were you ever, Wurt? I thought that was the core problem."

"I think it's fair to say that we had reached an accord," clarified Wurt, with a tone that suggested that this was a recent epiphany. "Now... no, it's no use..." As he spoke, Wurt withdrew his flask and now he gave it a demonstrative slosh. "...I can hardly bear the smell of the stuff."

"I say, Wurt, that's... Well, that's rather a jolly good thing, isn't it?"

"I'm afraid I don't follow, Mister Boisjoly."

"Why, it's just like Belter Belstead. Used to be a member of the Juniper until his wife made him quit."

"Most tragic..."

"Not quite there yet," I continued. "Belter had never shown an ounce of inspiration his entire life. Read Anthropology at university because the prospectuses were in alphabetical order. For years he had a standing order in the dining room for roast beef, Yorkshire pudding, potatoes, gravy, half bottle of Merlot. Married the first girl who gave him a dance at the débutante's ball, 1922 — his first, incidentally — and that's when everything changed. His wife made him take the cure, you see, and quit all his clubs, so that he had nowhere to get a drink."

"I see." Wurt rubbed his chin comprehendingly.

"Almost there," I assured him. "This development cracked open a vein of heretofore undiscovered enterprise in Belter. He became very active in the temperance movement, and founded an organisation for men just like himself — the Sobriety League."

"I understand, Mister Boisjoly." Wurt nodded with solemn understanding.

"Exactly," I confirmed. "The Sobriety League was a private drinking club. It's as though the man saved up all his ingenuity and splashed out on one revolutionary idea. Made a nice packet, too, until he had his first and last encounter with an escalator at Earl's Court."

"Oh."

"Yes, quite," I agreed. "The moral lesson probably resonates a bit more if you edit out that last bit. Is that the dinner bell I hear?"

"There is a buffet in the dining room, in light of the indefinite number of guests."

"Excellent." I rubbed my hands together in anticipation. "I look forward to seeing how thinly Prax manages to spread a mashed turnip."

It was in the poorest of taste, it was in the best of taste.

With Cecil's departure, it would appear, famine had ended and the feast instantered. Despite the vexes and vitriol and violent demise, the mediaeval dining room of Carnaby Castle was a cosy theatre of chatter and cheer. There was a high fire in the great inglenook in which Prax was basting several fat pheasants. Lint conscripted Wurt into carvery service while she crowded the vast table with baked bird, fidgety pie, boulders of crusty bread, marbley sage cheese, grilled root vegetables stewed in cream, and pitchers of golden cider.

No one was missing out. Barnaby and Cressida were consoling a brooding Win next to the fire, holding plates in one hand and balancing their glasses on a stool between them. Carnaby was listening with his signature blank stare to something that Bunty was urgently explaining, complete with broad illustrative gesticulations describing the motions of the planets, dashing potatoes from her plate with each orbit. Aloof from them in that way the truly spiritual tend to be in groups was Wandalen, eating a leg of pheasant with her hands. Hovering suspiciously by the door but nevertheless dining like rescued sailors were Ivor and Constable Blewit.

I say no one was missing out. Everyone was enjoying what doubtless was one of Prax's *chef-d'oeuvres,* except a certain short-sighted Londoner who had rather overdone it at the Towny Castle Pub dinner buffet. I made an effort, but I barely had room for a slice of roast pheasant, couple of potatoes and gravy, small helping of stewed turnip and, possibly later, a fist of bread and knob of cheese. Only time would tell.

The window rattled and drummed with thunder and rain in insistent contradiction to the warm plenty within. Lightning stroboscoped the glass and a whistling wind made several successful incursions by the chimney, causing the fire to woosh and wobble and the lamplight on the walls to flicker in time.

"What ho, wallflowers," I said to the honour guard at the door. "Not mingling? Speaking for myself, I haven't seen such a festive wake since poor Papa's seeing-off, and my mother had been planning that for months."

"Must hold the official line, Mister Boisjoly," replied Blewit in a confidential tone.

"You don't mean..."

"Yes. We shall be making an arrest shortly," precipitated Ivor.

"We'd be on our way with our man already," confided Blewit. "But Gordy won't start in the wet."

"Our man? One accusative masculine singular, for both murders?"

"There's only one viable suspect without an alibi in both cases." Ivor spoke in a duck hunter's whisper.

"Carnaby the club steward," I supposed in hushed tones. "My mind always dazzles when talk turns to legal technicalities, Inspector — will a trial be necessary?"

Ivor regarded me wearily from beneath hooded eyes while he dispatched a mouthful of pheasant. "I assume you want to stick your oar in."

"I'm touched by how well you know me."

Blewit had observed this exchange with growing excitement, and keeping to form delivered this next line as though it was a show-stopping punchline; "Just to keep it straight, Inspector, am I still arresting Carnaby?"

And, indeed, it was a show-stopper. The rhythmic din of a talkative standup dinner party came to a sharp-edged halt, and a clap of thunder shook the window frame.

"To which Carnaby do you refer, Constable?" asked Cressida, after an awkward silence.

"Yes, Inspector, that's the question, isn't it?" I pointed out. "Certainly there's a killer among the Carnabys, but there are so many from which to choose."

"We shall be requiring Mister Wselfwulf Carnaby to assist us in our enquiries," announced Ivor with that talent for stiff euphemism that comes so naturally to the British detecting class.

"Oh, that's a very good idea," said Bunty. "Wselfwulf's ever so clever, aren't you Wselfwulf?"

"They mean they think that Uncle Wself is the killer, Bunty," explained Cressida.

"Who did he kill?" asked Bunty, and then took a bite of fidgety pie.

"I think, in light of the absence of corroborating accounts of his activities, the inspector believes Wselfwulf to be responsible for both murders," I explained.

"Both murders?" marvelled Bunty. "Who else has died?"

"Still only Cecil and Ludovica, but the inspector holds to the narrow-minded view that Ludovica was not, in fact, carried off by the mists."

"Nonsense," dismissed Bunty. "What possible reason could Wselfwulf have to murder anyone?"

"Yes, how about that, Inspector?" I asked. "If your theory is that Carnaby killed Cecil because he loved Ludovica, then why ever would he have killed Ludovica?"

"I say, steady on, Anty," stuttered Carnaby, with all the fluent ease of one reading an eye chart.

"Come, come, Carnaby," I urged. "Now is no time for false graces. Far more scandalous truths than that will be soon spoken about you in a public courtroom by a king's counsel who knows little to nothing of your skill with a syphon. Might not even be a whisky drinker."

"There are other motives for murder," pointed out Ivor.

"Oh, loads, right in this very room," I agreed. "Carnaby, for instance, may well have wanted to return to his role as castle patriarch."

"The truth is, I never enjoyed the privilege," claimed Carnaby. "I was very happy to relinquish the responsibility."

"And I know you to be a man with an irreproachable sense of duty," I said. "So maybe you did Cecil in to protect the rest of the family from his sinister plan to starve them out of the castle."

"Oh, thank you, Wselfwulf," beamed Bunty. She popped a nugget of Derby Sage into her mouth.

"Or you, Bunty," I continued. "Your dispute with Cecil was a matter of life and death — yours."

"I don't know what you mean."

"No one fears the curse more than you, Bunty," I explained. "And Cecil terminated your principal protection when he cancelled the arrangement with Miss Kettle."

"He didn't even believe there was a curse."

"He lived a sheltered life," I said in defence of the deceased. "Perhaps you killed Cecil out of fear for your own."

"Make up your mind, Boisjoly," seethed Win. "Who killed my father?"

"I'm afraid you're going to have to be more specific, Win — to which father do you refer?"

"Cecil, of course."

"Well, how do we know it wasn't you?" I asked.

"Me? Why would I kill him?"

"For one thing," I explained. "You persist in this contention that he was your legal father, which would make you sole known beneficiary to the fortune he would have inherited from Ludovica. You're wrong, of course, but the motive stands."

"You don't seriously think I believed Cecil to be my father in any legal sense," said Win.

"Just a second," interjected Cressida. "What fortune?"

"Ludovica was a very wealthy woman," I explained.

"Because she killed my father," insisted Win.

"She was dead already," pointed out Cressida.

"My real father."

"Well, I'm lost," declared Cressida.

"It's quite simple, Sid," claimed Barnaby. "Win's real father — who was quite wealthy — was married to Ludovica, who eventually murdered him making her, in turn, quite wealthy. Later, she married Uncle Cecil. When she was fetched up by the curse, Cecil inherited her fortune."

"Then who killed Cecil?" asked Cressida.

"Who's to say it wasn't you or Barnaby?" I proposed. "Or, more convincingly, both of you."

"You overestimate me, Anty old chap," said Barnaby with the suave modesty of a Saint James Park swan.

"You know, I don't think I do, Nobs," I replied. "Cecil positioned the sword of Damocles over both your heads — if something weren't done, and done quickly, you were facing a fate that was anathema to your very philosophy — you were going to have to work for a living."

"No!"

"Yes!" I countered, accompanied by a whip-crack of lightning at the window. "But with Cecil out of the way, you would continue to live the charade of privilege, until you or the charade of privilege got old."

"Do them nothing but good," commented Lint, much in the nature of a dam bursting.

"I can only take your word on that," I said. "Of course, Cecil's departure doesn't do you any harm either, does in Lint?"

"Don't see how it helps."

"Of course you do. Cecil's return to Hoy reset the clock on your long, linty vigil for the time when Castle Carnabys are no more, or at any rate are no more in Hoy. With Cecil gone and the fortunes of the family dwindling, you could finally realise your dream of turning the castle into an hotel and fishing resort."

"Fishing resort? Who said anything about a fishing resort?" asked Lint.

"I added that bit," I confessed. "Spiffing idea, though."

"He's not wrong." Ivor added his vote of support.

At this point the door opened, freeing a current of air trapped in the chimney to exhale into the room and stoke the flames in the inglenook and shudder the lamps. The dining room went dark and the fire blazed and the contrast created a flash of blindness. When, a moment later, the flames and torches settled, Odd was among us.

"Ah, Odd," I said, for I expected this development. "You are among us at last."

"What is *he* doing here?" sniffed Wandalen.

"I took the liberty of inviting him," I replied. "I thought if the Castle Pub had to be closed this evening, it was only fair that the Castle Pub be closed, too."

"I don't want any trouble, Wandalen." Odd raised his palms in peace and put his back to the door.

"Of course you do, Odd," I said. "In fact, factional conflict has been your bread and butter for years, and you and Wandalen have colluded in maintaining it."

"Colluded? Me and Wandalen?" scoffed Odd.

"Collusion, if anything, is an understatement," I said. "Perhaps 'passionate affair' is closer to the mark. Publicly, you fuel the flames of partisanship which neatly divides the trade of the discerning tippler. Privately, you meet for secret picnics in the mausoleums of the cemetery, using separate accesses to the catacombs and leaving behind chicken bones, chalices, and adolescent doodles that I initially took for evidence of witchery ritual."

"You're guessing at that which you cannot possibly understand." Wandalen gazed at me over a menacing drumstick. "There is only one Castle Pub in Hoy."

"That's right," agreed Odd.

"Certainly your suppliers think so," I said. "Resulting in substantial savings, I expect, when your beer comes from the same barrel and your cheddar the same block."

"How could you know that?" marvelled Odd.

"It's a gift," I said. "Now, there's nothing very wrong with any of this — not really in keeping with what Adam Smith would recognise as the spirit of the free market, but what is? However Cecil's crusade against the dark arts as alternative to paying rent and his assault on the rivalry on which your business model is based — that amounts to a very good motive, in so far as there is such a thing, for murder."

"Odd..." Torchlight flickered on Wandalen's face as she gazed warm fuzzies at the barkeep of her affections. "...would never hurt anyone."

"I'm just glad our truth is finally known." Odd smiled vacantly at the witch who enchanted his heart. "Honestly, I believe the crypt was giving me rheumatism."

An uncomfortable silence followed this, as we waited for the two now liberated lovers to sweep across the room into one another's arms. When that didn't happen, Wurt seized the spotlight.

"You forgot about me, Mister Boisjoly — I'd have happily killed Cecil Carnaby."

"Oh, I know you would have, Wurt," I assured him. "To stop him taking from you the one thing you truly loved."

"Cecil tried to come between Wurt and whisky?" It was Cressida who spoke but there was a general gape and awe.

"Well, that settles that," declared Barnaby.

"No, not whisky," I clarified. "If Wurt murdered Cecil, it was to protect Bunty."

"Bunty?" said Bunty. "Whatever do you mean?"

"You were Wurt's first and only thought when he learned of Cecil's plan to scatter the contents of Castle Carnaby to the four winds," I said.

"Is this true, Wurt?" asked Bunty.

"I believe it was the cause of my affliction, madam."

In reply Bunty chewed meditatively on a crust of pie.

"Leaving us, finally, with Prax," I said.

"Me? I had nothing against Cecil," claimed Prax.

"No?" I asked. "Then perhaps he had something against you. Cecil was known to pass considerable time in the cemetery, ostensibly researching his memoir."

"So?" Prax affected to be distracted by a particularly delicate basting challenge. "Nothing to do with me."

"Unless, while studying the crypts and cenotaphs, Cecil were to discover something that could cost you your position in the community."

"Did Cecil discover something about Prax?" asked Cressida.

"Not really my place to say," I said. "But it does round out the list of possible motives."

"Very well, Mister Boisjoly." Ivor, who had employed my discourse to clear his plate, set it on the table and took out his pipe. "You've established that everyone had a motive to kill Cecil Carnaby, but that doesn't change the fact that only one person could have done it. Constable?"

Blewit washed down a crust of bread with a draught of cider, drew his journal from his pocket, and flipped backwards through time.

"At approximately ten minutes before ten yesterday evening, Inspector Wittersham, Mister Boisjoly, and myself overheard a violent confrontation from within the bedroom of the late Ludovica Carnaby. We gained entry and found the deceased, Mister Cecil Carnaby. The room was otherwise empty, but the back of the fireplace was open, revealing a secret passage."

Blewit paused for a stabilising draw on his cider, wiped his mouth with his sleeve, and continued.

"An exhaustive search of the passage established that four other rooms could be accessed from the scene of the crime."

"You went through Cecil's room," Ivor reminded me. "And it was empty."

"Confirmed."

"I encountered Mister Boisjoly in the passage," recounted Blewit. "This was on the second-floor landing. I saw no one other than Mister Boisjoly."

"And then you proceeded to the first floor, where you first encountered, I believe, Mrs Stokely and Miss Kettle," continued Ivor.

"Correct again," I said. "The main hall, first floor, north side, appears to be nothing but your normal linen closets, service rooms, and temples to the dark arts. Prax and Miss Kettle were realigning the twaddletips of the restored amulet. I expect direct exposure to the scepticism of the metropolitan cynic plays all sorts of havoc with its powers."

Blewit turned a page of his notebook to remind himself, "Mrs Stokely had sent the butler to fetch Miss Wandalen Kettle at about quarter after nine. Miss Kettle and Wurt returned to the castle at roughly quarter to ten, when Miss Kettle joined Mrs Stokely for the, ehm..."

"Resanctifying," decreed Wandalen, then, in reply to Blewit's pained expression, added, "Just say ceremony."

"You then proceeded to the only other room accessible from the first-floor passage — the linen closet." Ivor spoke to me during the official lighting of the detecting pipe.

"Taxonomically correct, but it was very spacious. More of a linen stockpile."

"The maid, who had just then provided me with the key, arrived at the same moment," puffed Ivor. "Prax was already there."

"To the smallest detail," I concurred.

Blewit resumed the narrative at this point, "Barnaby Carnaby was with Cressida in her room. They both heard the maid and the door to the linen closet open and close. At this point, Barnaby remembered that he was bringing cocktails to Elwin Trewsbury, consequently he and Elwin were witness to Mister Boisjoly announcing the murder."

"I read the room," I explained. "The air was eighty-three percent anticipation, and expectations were running high."

"That leaves the butler, who arrived from the ground floor at about this time, confirmed by Cressida, who opened her door and also heard Mister Boisjoly." Ivor all but dusted off his hands at this point. "For my part, I proceeded to the only other room accessible via the passage from the scene of the crime — that of Wselfwulf Carnaby."

"And of course, he was alone," I added, helpfully.

"He was." Ivor paused for effect and, for a bit of atmosphere, to tease a stout stratocumulus from his pipe. "Among those who had access to the room in which the murder was committed, Wselfwulf Carnaby was once again the only one without an alibi."

"Damning case, Inspector, deftly stated," I ceded. "But this only addresses opportunity and, by extension, means, but what of the motive?"

"As you've already established, Mister Boisjoly, Wselfwulf Carnaby had a strong motive to murder his cousin Cecil."

"*A* motive, yes," I specified. "I'm referring to *the* motive."

"And what is *the* motive?"

"I should have thought that would be obvious, Inspector," I said. "Cecil Carnaby was murdered because he killed Ludovica Carnaby."

CHAPTER TWENTY

The Mystery of the Missing Memoir

At this point the storm stepped up its efforts to join the party. The window frame rattled with thunder and the panes crackled with arcs of sparks. The wind whistled in the chimney and pushed into the dining room and openly menaced the oil lamps. Ivor's pipe went out.

"We've been over this, Boisjoly," said Ivor between rekindling puffs, "Wselfwulf Carnaby is the only one who can't account for his activities at the time of the death of Ludovica."

"Actually, he can," I countered. "It's true that, among those on the grounds, he was the only one who was alone during the murder, but he was seen at the castle some ten minutes later. We know that Ludovica was actually killed at the bottom of the cliff and, while Carnaby is certainly the only one who could have made it *to* the scene of the crime by then, he could never have made it back."

"Beg your pardon, sir," interjected Blewit, who had been leafing to a pertinent passage in his notebook, "neither could have Cecil Carnaby. He was seen at the cemetery some ten minutes after Mrs Carnaby was last seen on the top of the scarp."

"By Prax Carnaby, from the south tower, Wandalen Kettle, from the Castle Pub, and by Win Trewsbury, who was also in the graveyard at the time," I said. "I know. And yet, minutes before, he had murdered his wife with a rock."

"Impossible to cover that distance in that time on foot," asserted Ivor.

"Absolutely impossible," I agreed. "By boat, however, on a rushing river, he had time to spruce up a little, taking into account about ten extra seconds before the sun sets in the lowlands of Hoy."

"Boat..."

"Boat," I confirmed. "Fishing is excellent around here, I'm told, and done all over. There's a little pier at the bottom of the scarp, and a mooring beneath the bridge next to the cemetery. Between them, I'm reliably informed, the river rapidly races. As Barnaby and Lint arrived at the top of the scarp, Cecil floated around the bend. Moments later, as Prax peered out from the balcony of the south tower, he moored beneath the bridge next to the graveyard."

"Of course," realised Ivor.

"In preparation for his diabolical plan he tied up a little skiff at the foot of the scarp. Then he arranged to meet his wife for one of their secret little picnics..."

"What secret little picnics?" asked Ivor. "No one mentioned anything about secret picnics?"

"That's because they were secret," I explained. "A romantic practice that Cecil put in place on arrival at the castle. He would schedule a tryst with his wife somewhere on the grounds — the bottom of the scarp, for instance — and then retire to 'work on his memoir' which, I noticed when I was in his room earlier, doesn't exist."

"That's..." Blewit flipped a page of his notebook. "...true."

"The rendez-vous were sufficiently frequent that Cressida, in her role as chief espionage officer, concluded that Ludovica was carrying on a secret affair. She was, it turns out, but it was with her husband."

Blewit snapped a page of his notepad and stabbed it with a stubby index finger.

"Elwin Trewsbury," he read aloud.

"Yes, Constable?" encouraged Ivor.

"Mister Trewsbury was seen in the graveyard at the same time as Cecil Carnaby," Blewit paraphrased from his notes. "He might just as easily have murdered Ludovica Carnaby, the woman he believes killed his father, and covered the distance in time by boat, just as you said."

"I was in the catacombs," protested Win.

"So we understand," agreed Ivor. "However, as I've seen with my own eyes, an underground river flows directly beneath the castle — all the way to the cemetery."

"I considered that, to my regret," I regretted. "It's why I was there when someone developed a pressing need to lock me in. During my calm, measured analysis of the venue, I discovered that the walls weep constantly, as though for the timeless dead in their care. Or, more in keeping with current thinking in geology circles, the catacombs are below the water line — if they could access the river they'd be entirely flooded."

Ivor expelled an acquiescent cloud of smoke. Blewit watched him.

"I suppose you know why Cecil Carnaby murdered his wife," assumed, correctly, Ivor.

"For her money."

"For my father's money," corrected Win.

"Plus that of her previous husband," I calculated for everyone's benefit.

"But, they were married in Italy," pointed out Ivor. "Why bring her all the way to Hoy just to kill her?"

"Home field advantage, partially," I said. "But mainly because he wasn't planning on killing her himself. He hoped that the curse would do it."

"He didn't believe in the curse," Bunty reminded us.

"I think that he was undecided," I countered. "He had hopes that the curse would do his dirty work or, failing that, one of you would."

"He thought that one of us was going to kill his wife for him?" Cressida laughed with amateur-theatrics derision, and the storm echoed her with a thunderous guffaw.

"Well, you very nearly did, didn't you?" I said this distracted by the cheese board, which had been teasing my interest for some time. I continued my thought while separating two inches of cheddar from the mother brick and claiming a crunchy crust of bread. "Or, at any rate, you prepared for the eventuality, starting with sending Uncle Wselfwulf that cryptic cable at the Juniper."

"How absurd." Barnaby mimicked his sister's stagey scoff. "Why ever would we have done such a thing?"

"Oh, Nobby." Cressida massaged her brow.

"What? What have I said?"

"Your sister is exasperated, Barnaby, by what amounts to a confession," I elucidated. "I didn't say anything about both of you."

"Ah."

"Ah, indeed," I confirmed. "When Cecil cabled to say that he was arriving with a new bride, and that things were going to change here at Castle Carnaby, you prepared a diabolical plan B. First, you sent a telegram to Wselfwulf with a worrying message that he couldn't resist, to ensure that he was on hand to enlarge the field of suspects."

"Suspects? Suspects of what?" Barnaby wanted to know.

"The attempts on Cressida's life, and the eventual successful removal of Ludovica," I said.

"Oh, there were never any attempts on my life," said Cressida with a can-we-change-the-subject-now off-handedness.

"No," I agreed. "They were staged. Clumsily, too, I might add. In fact, I believe I will add that they were clumsily staged to appear as though someone — probably Uncle Wselfwulf — was helping the curse to manifest its destiny."

"It was more of a precaution, Anty. You understand." Barnaby waved away the miscellany of murder while his sister applied both hands to the increasingly demanding task of massaging her brow.

"Nobby, why don't you eat something sticky," suggested Cressida.

"In fact, Sid, it's not your brother who gave the game away," I said. "It was you."

"How so?"

"To be entirely frank, I found the series of improbably near misses suspicious from the outset," I recounted. "For instance, the rampart which gave up the ghost over the very spot where, you claimed, you have your after-dinner cigarette."

"Oh, dear."

"Yes," I agreed. "Yesterday you told me that you were able to keep such a sharp eye on Ludovica because you take said digestive expectorant on the allure, atop the south wall. The occasion in which you were locked in the wine cellar was hardly a grave menace to your life — you probably had a key and in any case you knew that you wouldn't have to wait long for Wurt to do one of his famous inventories. As for the creosote fire I confess — I don't know how that was done."

"That was real," admitted Cressida. "It's what gave us the idea — like Nobby says, it was just a precaution."

"In case you needed to murder Ludovica Carnaby."

"Yes. I mean, no..."

"In any case," I mercifully redirected. "Cecil lost patience with you or the curse, and took matters into his own hands. Doubtless that was always the backup plan, and it's why he instituted the rotating system of romantic rendez-vous, an arrangement in which Ludovica delighted, for reasons which will shortly become clear. Cecil hoped, at best, that you would incriminate yourselves, and you very nearly did."

"Yes, well, we shall have to consider what other charges may need to be made," said Ivor. "Let us proceed, though, with the hypothesis that Cecil murdered his wife who was, as you say, subsequently avenged. Presumably by one of the gentlemen present in this room."

Ivor led a parade of suspicious glances from Win, to Carnaby, to Barnaby.

Barnaby took this in and stuttered into action. "Ah, well, I see how some things I've said might have been taken to imply that there was something... something of a romantic nature between Ludovica and myself, but the whole affair... I don't mean affair, of course, the whole, sort of, let us say, exchange, was more along the courtly lines, if you will. A chivalrous regard from afar."

"I'm quite certain that's true, Inspector," I translated. "Barnaby's passions are of a higher plane; more... lofty, noble, perhaps... imaginary! That's the word I want — imaginary. He wasn't having any sort of affair with Ludovica."

"And it certainly weren't Elwin Trewsbury, Inspector," asserted the constable, anchoring a passage in his notepad with a thick thumb. "He hated Ludovica Carnaby, on account of her murdering his father."

"I think we can take it, Constable, that no potential suspect can be taken at his word," said Ivor.

"Oh, no, Inspector," I differed. "On this point I think we can assume that Win is quite sincere and, in my view, quite correct — Ludovica Carnaby, formerly Ludovica Trewsbury, formerly Ludovica Birkit, formerly Ludovica Gaggiano, murdered at least her previous two husbands. Furthermore, she planned to murder Cecil Carnaby."

"What? Why?"

"For *his* money."

"Did he have any money?"

"Not a sausage," I estimated. "Although he would have everyone think otherwise, particularly his wife, who was allowed to believe that he had amassed a fortune shovelling things about, and that this castle was his to control, once he ridded it of an infestation of kin."

"Aspinall's!" contributed Odd.

"Exactly, Odd. Aspinall's."

"Who or what is Aspinall's?" asked Ivor.

"Jeweller's in Bond Street," I replied.

"A very fine jeweller's," completed Odd.

"Thank you, Odd," I said. "A very fine jeweller's, from whom Cecil bought gifts for his wife on credit."

"So, Cecil Carnaby posed as a castled landowner to attract a wealthy wife, whom he would then murder," summarised Ivor. "Bit of a stretch from that to Ludovica making her living murdering husbands."

"It would be," I acknowledged. "If we didn't have what amounts to a confession from her accomplice." I paused for an operatic thunderclap. "Win Trewsbury murdered his father." The thunder sustained a rumbling, cinematic accompaniment. "Both of them."

CHAPTER TWENTY-ONE

Luckily Armed With a Lucky Charm

"You…" growled Win, struggling for just the right epithet.

"Maestro?" I suggested. "Prodigy? Marvel? Feel free to speak your mind, Win. I've heard it all before and I have a very thick skin."

"You… are next!" Win exploded and in the same instant so, too, did the storm. A flash and a crash burst at the window, a small tornado billowed down the chimney, the lamps blew out and the fire blew up, and Win took hold of the kettle hook pinioned to the chimney and yanked it, as though to use it as a weapon. It didn't come away, though, and its creaking groan added to the general chaos as the entire left side of the inglenook receded with a sharp scrape of stone on stone. Win leapt over the fire and disappeared into the hidden passage.

"After him, Constable," ordered Ivor, while vaulting like a gazelle over the dining table, sweeping away the ginger parkin before I even got a fork in. He paused at the inglenook, glanced quickly about, selected a stout rolling pin, and disappeared in pursuit of Win.

Blewit stared after him wide-eyed, doubtless reflecting with strong emotions on the time he spent hovering over a yawning chasm of saw-toothed death.

"Prax — take Constable Blewit to the most likely exit," I said, and followed Ivor into the darkness.

The passage at this point was very much an extension of the inglenook. It was high and wide for a fireplace but awkwardly low and narrow for the scene of a dramatic chase. It was also dark and heavy with lingering smoke. Visibility was poor.

Hence when the inspector stopped at a fork in the road I collided with him.

"Where's Blewit?" asked Ivor with hushed urgency.

"Point duty," I explained. "We took a vote in your absence."

"Very well. I expect he went this way." Ivor probably gestured in the dark. "It appears to lead toward the courtyard and the town. I'll follow. Have a look down that way. If you see him, call out for help. If he tries to escape, let him."

"Count on me, Inspector."

We separated at the fork. I took a sharp left and knew that I was circumnavigating the kitchen, and in a few feet I was within the thick external wall of the castle. Here, again, the passage divided. Following the inspector's logic, I went right, guessing that it was more in keeping with the instincts of a fugitive from justice, however I immediately came to some stairs and a late epiphany.

I turned back the other way and moved as swiftly as I could manage in what was now complete darkness. There was a beacon, though, in the form of the storm, which rattled and moaned progressively more loudly as I felt my way forward. Presently a crisp blast of white light illuminated a doorway ahead and an instant later I was looking out a narrow postern that, from the outside, would have appeared a long-ago walled-up sentry post at the back of the castle. A long, twisted finger of lightning traced from the low clouds into the gorge and briefly lit a scene fittingly misty and wet, with a dense veil of vapour rising beyond the scarp. I reached into my jacket and gripped my lucky charm, and then proceeded into the tempest.

I had no real plan. I had, rather, the opposite of a plan. I planned to do nothing and observe. Specifically, I intended to race to the scarp and verify my suspicion that Win had prepared for all of this with a skiff tied up at the bottom of the scarp. I estimated that I had just enough time.

What I didn't have was visibility. The stairs down the cliffside disappeared into the mist. Win was gone, and I knew that even with my lucky charm there was no way that I could muster the will to pursue him. Even as I tried to stare through the mist, it grew denser and greyer and it rose in self-perpetuating billows until soon it was rolling over the edge of the scarp and enveloping me. I turned back toward the castle and couldn't see it.

"You are next!"

Win's huge, hazy form silhouetted before me, like a shadow-theatre for bears.

"Ah, what ho, Win." I tightly gripped my lucky charm and spoke with according confidence. Win approached and I could make out his grim, determined features.

I didn't then and I don't now believe in lucky charms. However, earlier in the evening, as I was dressing for dinner, I realised that I had yet to return Constable Blewit's billy club, and I regarded that fact to be very lucky indeed. I withdrew it, then, and tested the heft of my lucky charm against my palm. It felt very lucky.

"I warn you, Win, I'm armed." I held up the billy club to illustrate the point. "I further warn you that I'm quite terrified and subject to sudden movements and erratic behaviour."

I blame the fog for what happened next. It was concentrated pea soup at that point and depth perception was largely a matter of guesswork. Win dodged and I swung and missed the target by something between an inch and a yard and a half. I saw nothing but fog for a moment when the lightning again illuminated the scene and a monstrous shadow appeared at my side and relieved me of my lucky charm.

This time it was my turn to dodge or, put more accurately, it was my turn to slip in the mud the moment that Win brought the billy club down. Win pressed his advantage, and I slithered like a lizard in the mire and mist until I realised that I'd pushed myself partially over the edge of the cliff.

Win appeared over me as a mist-monster, enrobed in a miasma of angry grey. He raised the club for a fatal blow that could only be avoided by pushing myself off the scarp.

In the instant of indecision, a piercing screech came to us, slicing through the mist and the night and the fear and my inner ear. Win started and swung at a black wraith that came at him from nowhere and everywhere and, as he looked up, he was raised up.

In my recollection, the events which next unfolded occurred over several minutes, with short intermission. In reality, it was probably less than a second during which Win, distracted by Buns the crow, must have lost his footing and pitched over the edge of the scarp.

CHAPTER TWENTY-TWO

The Twist in the Mist

It was one of those disoriented, disjointed, disconnected mornings in which one dreamily tries to sort out where one is. I drifted lightly into consciousness in my own deep, downy bed in Kensington. Then I fluttered up to the dizzying south tower of Carnaby Castle and shuddered briefly in the depths of the catacombs. Then I think I was at Eton, and Vickers was House Master, rousing me for parents' day.

"Good morning, sir. I have brought tea."

The morning sun spilt happily through the hole in the ceiling of my room in the attic of the Towny Castle Pub. Beyond it the sky was a cloudless cyan, and everything smelled of bacon. Vickers composed a resourceful construction of milking stool and breadboard next to my bed and handed me a perfumed pour of primer.

"I have laid out our tweed travelling suit."

"Morning, Vickers," I finally managed. "I take it Inspector Wittersham has delivered dateline Hoy."

"Not entirely, sir. I understand that the mysteries have been solved, and I took the liberty of presuming that we would be returning today to London." Vickers took a cockeyed view of the tweeds he'd draped over my open suitcase. "However the inspector gave me to understand that he wished to pose to you what he described as 'searching questions'."

"Yes, I don't doubt he does." I sipped my tea from the comfort of my straw mattress and observed Vickers' baffled analysis of my travel-wrapper. "One tie too many, Vickers, and not enough trousers. Otherwise, impeccable. Is the inspector downstairs?"

"Yes, sir. At breakfast. As are most of the occupants of the castle." Vickers, pursuing some strategy best left unexplored, set about repacking my suit. Possibly with a view to taking a running restart. "He implied that he was of a mind to refer further criminal charges."

The entire Carnaby collective was cluttered about the brimming breakfast buffet in the bar room. Prax and Lint shared a table and a selection of everything, including asparagus submerged in butter and kippers that I could probably have tasted at a hundred paces. As I arrived, Bunty was joining Wurt in the corner and placing before him a deep and dark tankard of coffee. Barnaby and Cressida disputed ownership of a choice slice of steak and kidney pie. Odd and Wandalen were restocking the tea and table, respectively, and recording the morning's credit on a slate.

"Good morning, Inspector." I joined Ivor at the bar, from whence he observed the frenzy from behind a screen of pipe smoke, armed with a cup of tea. "I notice a disturbing absence of lake trout from the breakfast *à la carte* — did you oversleep?"

"I had rather a lot to do at the castle, as you might well imagine."

"Yes, I apologise for that," I said without, frankly, meaning it. "You try to keep things casual and chatty but then, before you know it, someone's going over a cliff."

"Yes, about that… would you like to explain what happened?"

"I see what you're driving at, Inspector, and I suppose I might just as well come clean with you." I spoke in confidential tones. "It was dark and the rain raged and the fog was like a blindfold. We struggled at the top of the scarp, and Win Trewsbury had the better of me. It was him or me, I hope you understand that. I was forced to resort to an old trick taught me by my Uncle Evraud, who served in the royal dragoons, you know, which involves slipping in the mud and begging for mercy. Of course it worked, but at what cost?" I shook my head slowly. "What cost? Oh, thank you, Odd." I was rescued from despair by a timely cup of tea.

"Did he say anything?"

"No, but I would have thought that fleeing arrest and attempted murder amounted to something approaching a confession, or its near equivalent."

"It does." Ivor nodded absently into his personal pipe smoke stratosphere. "I assume you'd like to explain how you figured it out."

"I wouldn't like to, Inspector, no," I said. "You know how timid I am about my accomplishments, but I feel that the residents of Hoy would benefit from a full unveiling of the deep currents which flow beneath the hollow hill. If you'll join me at the buffet, I'll just strengthen the sinews for the reckoning."

The breakfast bounty was varied but I had much to say. I adhered mainly to the bacon, boiled egg, and crusty bread schools, and dabbled in tea. Ivor, I expect, had already eaten, as had Blewit, who was nevertheless making another careful study of the kippers, asparagus, and fried potato faction. I positioned myself at the pulpit of the buffet and addressed the assembly.

"The catalytic clue was the theme of façade, introduced so capably by Carnaby."

"Which Carnaby?" asked Ivor.

"Carnaby Carnaby," I replied. "The only Carnaby that I call Carnaby — chief steward of the Juniper Gentleman's Club."

"I say, what's all this, Anty?" Carnaby chuckled nervously.

"You might as well hear it now, Carnaby — your secret has been widely known throughout the castle and town for years," I said. "The only one who didn't know that you're a London club steward was Odd."

"I knew it," corrected Odd.

"Everybody knew it," I revised. "But you were far from alone in playing an ill-fitting role. Lint, for example, is no more a slovenly slob than she is a Castle Carnaby. Prax has her own secret, far more extraordinary than yours. Odd effects to be intimidated by witchcraft and Wandalen pretends to be a witch. Wurt drowns his true feelings for Bunty and Bunty imagines herself the living, lively, full-time preoccupation of a four hundred year old curse. I tried and, obviously, failed to pass myself off as your dimwitted disciple. The entire town of Hoy is playing opposite roles of privilege and poverty, when it's the townies with the strategic stockpiles of cheddar and fidgety pie and the castle Carnabys who barely eat and employ pickling alum as a cocktail mixer. Almost everyone was pretending to be someone or something that they're not, above all Cecil and Ludovica Carnaby."

"Cecil claimed to be wealthy, of course," recalled Ivor. "What was Ludovica's deceit?"

"Innocence, I should say, above all," I said. "She was, after all, a serial husband-slayer. Probably never mentioned it once."

"Yes, you were on the point of explaining that last night, if memory serves — how do you know she murdered her previous husbands?"

"The reflecting pool."

"What reflecting pool? You mean in the villa in Bergamo?"

"None other." My resistance failed me, at this point, and I paused for an entire rasher of bacon. Then another. "You see, the only one among us who wasn't pretending to be someone else was Win Trewsbury. All his stories were true — he was a mountain climber and horse-perturber and member of the Caterpillar Club — and he hadn't the imagination to re-invent himself. His false name was the single most common last name in the English-speaking world. He told, in the main, the truth, including the fact that his father had been poisoned and then drowned in the reflecting pool. He also told me that he hadn't seen his father in the years that he'd been married to Ludovica, and prior to his life in Bergamo — so how did he know there was a reflecting pool?" I took a dramatic bite of boiled egg. "He knew about it, of course, because he was there. He knew that his father didn't succumb to the poison and had to be drowned because it was Win who overpowered his father, and it was Win who drowned him."

"At best that only proves that Win Trewsbury killed his father, not that Ludovica was involved," contended Ivor.

"Ah, but we know that she was planning on killing Cecil, and that she had an accomplice in town," I countered. "We know the accomplice wasn't within the castle walls, so it must have been Win."

"Slow down, Boisjoly," cautioned Ivor. "How do we know all that?"

"We extrapolate," I explained, "from a watershed clue identified by Blewit."

"Eh? Me?" Blewit paused a soda biscuit mid-journey.

"You," I confirmed. "Incidentally, Blewit, I meant to ask you something of tremendous importance regarding your search of Ludovica's room immediately after the first murder."

"Yes?"

"Come mai hai capito una lettera d'una donna italiana a sua madre?"

"Ack," exclaimed Bunty, then in a stage whisper to Wurt she said, "He's doing it again."

"Still Italian, Bunty," I assured her. "I merely asked the constable however he came to understand a letter from an Italian woman to her mother."

"Why, I just read it... oh, yes, I see what you mean," grasped Blewit.

"Exactly. Just as Cicero's letters chronicled Rome in the days leading to the assassination of Caesar, Ludovica's laid out a conspiracy with her lover. The difference being — let us say the key difference because, really, the list is immense — is that Cicero requires translation. Ludovica, like Cicero, was an avid correspondent — that was clear from her dwindling stationery supply — but nothing had been taken to the post office in Chesterfield since Christmas. More tellingly, for reasons which I hope now are obvious, she wrote to her mother in English. She described every detail of her life at the castle — her picnics with her husband, the secret passages she'd discovered — she wrote letters telling her mother everything she would need to know to plan Cecil Carnaby's murder."

"And somehow got them to Trewsbury," surmised Ivor.

"They met in secret. On at least one occasion in the cemetery, where they were seen by Wurt. This was risky, though, so my guess is that they visited the cemetery separately, leaving notes for each other, and on this one occasion happened to be there at the same time."

"All in aid of planning to murder Cecil," concluded Ivor.

"Just so." I held up a confirmatory boiled egg. "Doubtless Ludovica was happy to humour Cecil's predilection for secret trysts for they presented wider opportunity for fatal accident. And when I told Win that there'd been a death at the castle, he assumed that Ludovica had profited from one such opportunity."

"And when I told him it was Ludovica who'd died, he must have realised the truth."

"Precisely, Inspector — Win was not a creative thinker, but he was a quick thinker. In that instant he knew who had killed Ludovica, so he claimed to blame her for his father's death, masking the motive for what he was about to do."

"Oh, dear." Vickers is always at his most lucid in the morning or, put more accurately, if he's ever lucid it's usually in the morning.

"Yes, Vickers," I confirmed. "The moment after learning that Ludovica had been killed, Trewsbury learned from you that I had solved it and that I was in the catacombs. It was he who locked me in so that he might have time to exact revenge."

"Then, why didn't he?" asked Ivor.

"He did, eventually," I replied. "But he hadn't counted on Buns the crow nor the fact that I hadn't actually figured out that it was Cecil who'd killed his wife. Once again, thinking quickly, he gained access to the castle by the simple ruse of pretending to believe that he belonged there, and his first priority was to search

Ludovica's room and destroy any letters, but as fate would have it, he was surprised in the act by the very person he had come to kill."

"Very well, then, Mister Boisjoly." Ivor affected to divide his interest between my narrative and knocking out his pipe into a stone ashtray. "How did Trewsbury get out of a locked room, when all the exits were other rooms, and all of them were occupied?"

"You won't like it," I warned.

"As I suspected." Ivor gave his pipe one last, meaningful tap, drew himself up, and surveyed the bar room. "Someone here allowed the killer to get away."

"Yes, Inspector," I confirmed. "You."

"Me?"

"Not just you," I added, as a friend. "You and Constable Blewit."

"I never saw him," claimed Blewit through a kippered mouthful.

"No, that's how he got past you," I explained. "I realised what must have happened when I pursued Win into the passage from the kitchen — he knew the shortest route out of the castle, because Ludovica had already mapped it out for him. He also would have known that the passage accessible from Ludovica's room was a cul-de-sac."

"Then, how...?"

"Oldest trick in the book, Inspector." I was guessing a bit, at this point — there may well be older tricks. I haven't even read the book. "He sat in the reading chair, from whence Cecil surprised me when I was in Ludovica's room, and waited until you pursued him into the passage. Then he simply walked out the door, shadowed Lint back to the first floor and, in the moment when I was surprising her in the linen closet, he slipped back into his room. This is why Barnaby and Cressida believed that they heard the door of the linen closet open and close, which it didn't — they heard Win returning to his room. Moments later, he opened the door again, and feigned surprise that Cecil had been killed."

"He hid?" Ivor was scandalised. "You're telling me he hid?"

"Can't always be awe and cunning, Inspector, but as mentioned, Win was a quick thinker — he opened the door to the passage, giving you the impression that you needed to dash after him, with little time to reflect."

The inspector returned to the now redundant practice of knocking out his pipe, and the tapping served as ominous accompaniment to the glowering glare he cast over the present Carnabys, castle and otherwise.

"Very well," he said at last, still tapping his pipe hollowly. "Happily, there are still plenty of crimes that need answering..." tap, tap, tap. "Fraud..." Ivor tapped meaningfully at Wandalen. "Interfering with a police investigation, at the very least..." Ivor turned his judgmental tapping on Barnaby and Cressida.

"Perhaps there's a solution, Inspector..." I caught Wandalen's eyes. "...that requires less bureaucracy..." I aimed my weighty regard at Nobby and Sid. "...and less time in prison."

"I doubt that very much, Boisjoly," said Ivor flatly. "But I'm listening."

"All Barnaby and Cressida want, I think, is a dose of what the practical classes call 'real life'," I said. "I'm told it does wonders for the profligate and idle. People recommend it to me all the time."

"Prison is real life," pointed out Ivor.

"So is work," I pointed right back, "and Barnaby and Cressida are both in possession of talents which transfer extraordinarily well from wasting their time in a mediaeval castle to a productive life in London."

"London?" echoed Nobby, who was equally echoed by Sid.

"Unless you have some objection, and, indeed, even if you have quite substantial objections," I said. "It's the largest market for innovative cocktail mixology and, if there's any musical theatre hiring harpsichordists, they'll be in London. In any case, with a reference from your uncle Wselfwulf, London's finest and most respected club steward, you'll be sorted out in no time. Your London accommodations won't be as grand and granite as Carnaby Castle, but do you know what is grand and granite? Prison."

"*Could* you get us situations in London, Uncle Wselfwulf?" asked Cressida.

Carnaby raised a curt and correct club steward eyebrow. "Of course I can."

"And with all the male Castle Carnabys retiring to London life," I continued, "there remains no one to claim the last bequest of Ranaulf Carnaby meaning, if I understand correctly, it becomes community property."

"It does," confirmed Ivor.

"Just like that?" asked Lint.

"No more Castle Carnabys?" specified Prax.

"Just like that," I confirmed. "The castle is free to seek its destiny as a destination, offering the unparalleled beauty of the Peak District in the form of fields, feasts, fishing, and folk tales. Feel free to use that in the brochure."

"But, where will I go?" asked Bunty.

"You'll stay right where you are, Mrs Stokely," assured Lint. "We'll always take care of you."

"Perhaps you can even find in this an opportunity to engage with the world, or at least the village," I said to Bunty but addressed Wurt.

"But, the curse…" objected Bunty.

"Yes, the curse…" I assumed the bearing of a King's Counsel, and held up an authoritative strip of bacon. "Yesterday, Wandalen, I revisited the catacombs, and therein I discovered your secret."

"I don't know what you're talking about." Wandalen, who was engaged in the transportation and distribution of tea in that moment, tried and failed to appear disinterested.

"Then allow me to explain," I persisted. "I found the remains of Ravena Sooter."

"I knew it," claimed Bunty. "But how did you find her?"

"By working backwards," I explained. "It's been long rumoured that, four hundred years ago, Ravena Sooter was secretly placed in the catacombs, and that turns out to be true, but it's not the end of the story, is it Wandalen?"

The witch of Hoy fiddled idly with a tea cosy. "No."

"No," I repeated, for the benefit of the jury. "Ravena Sooter isn't alone. All of her descendants are there with her including, Wandalen, your mother."

"Then, Wandalen is..." Bunty took hold of her amulet with both hands.

"A direct descendent of Ravena Sooter," I announced. "And hence competent and qualified to lift the curse which has plagued this family for hundreds of years."

This was followed by a satisfyingly dramatic silence, something between that which precedes the Prince's final words in *Romeo and Juliet* and that which follows the dropping of a silver tray onto a marble floor at Claridge's, tea time.

"Then, why didn't you?" Bunty displayed a heretofore hidden talent for the obvious.

"Because the curse was good business," I explained. "It sustained tribal loyalties for the two Castle pubs, and it made for a lucrative sideline in charms and amulets."

"There may have been a bit of that." Wandalen spoke vaguely, ostensibly distracted by a tea ball she bobbled idly in a pot. "But mainly I was just giving back to the community — the curse has been part of the fabric of Hoy for four hundred years."

"It doesn't have to end here and now," I proposed. "Not entirely, at any rate. You could simply reform the curse — instead of a haunting, hunting affliction on the future of the Carnaby family name, the mist can be a harbinger of good fortune."

"Yes," delighted Bunty. "Do that one."

"I'll bet you it would work straight away," I said. "For instance Blewit and Inspector Wittersham would probably instantly lose interest in investigating anyone for obtaining money or goods by means of deception."

"Yes." Wandalen nodded thoughtfully. "A most worthy suggestion, Mister Boisjoly." She ceased bobbing the tea ball and instead opened it and turned the damp leaves onto a china saucer. She swished them about a bit, then removed her amulet and swayed it over the silt. "I hereby withdraw the Carnaby Castle Curse."

I traded on my restored reputation in the village of Hoy to organise a generous bun tythe for Buns the crow, and informed him of this arrangement while Vickers and Blewit loaded Gordy with luggage and an awkwardly large block of cheddar. Minutes later, we were bouncing painfully toward the train station in Chesterfield.

"That worked out well," announced Blewit, once he'd shifted us up to bruising speed. "I don't know how Gordy and me could have managed if we'd had to arrest everyone."

Ivor, who once again had taken the passenger seat, looked at the constable beneath bemused brows.

"There was never any risk of that, Constable."

"Eh?"

"The inspector and I had an arrangement," I explained. "I would propose happy solutions that placed no stress on our overburdened legal system and poor Gordy, and Inspector Wittersham would bring to bear the authoritative incentive of a warrant card issued by Scotland Yard."

"Oh, right," twigged Blewit. "Very clever Mister Boisjoly, Inspector." He paused to steer the two wheels on my side of the car over a deep pothole. "What I still don't understand, I think, is how you come to identify Ravena Sooter, after all these years, and her descendants, in the catacombs."

"Again, Constable, that was a ruse," I said with the staccato voice of thirty miles an hour over unmaintained Roman cobblestones. "I entirely invented the device of Wandalen Kettle's lineage to Ravena Sooter."

"Oh, of course." Blewit laughed at his late arrival to the party. "It's a wonder then that she was able to reverse the curse, isn't it?"

"I think that she was rather playing along at that point, Constable." I caught Ivor's amused eye in the rear-view mirror. "There never was a curse."

"But, the stories, Ravena Sooter, all those women fetched up…" protested Blewit.

"Ravena Sooter, like Wandalen Kettle, was an opportunist," I explained. "Had Ranulf Carnaby's new wife not bore him a son, he'd have never heard from her again. The subsequent deaths by violence are almost certainly exaggerations of the conflict that resulted in the division between town and castle Carnabys, and in fact the only actual recorded victim of the fog, we now know, was a hoax. As was the curse itself."

"Oh, I don't know about that, Mister Boisjoly." Blewit assumed a serious tone. "There's certainly something mystical in those mists — saved your life after all."

"It certainly appeared that way from where I lay," I admitted. "But, no, Win Trewsbury simply slipped and fell."

"That's not how your steward, Wselfwulf Carnaby tells it."

"Carnaby? What does he know of it — he was with you in the kitchen at the time."

"Oh, no sir." Blewit swerved to avoid missing a log. "He followed you into the passage. Says he got to you just as the crow called out — too late to help, but by then the mists were already fetching up Mister Trewsbury. Then they carried him right over the edge, so says Wselfwulf Carnaby."

To my recollection, Buns had called out just before Win lost his balance. Or just before he was raised up as though, indeed, by the mists, or by the hand of London's finest club steward who, I always maintained, would never kill, except in the course of duty.

The sun was high in a cloudless sky and all around us was the glimmering green and shimmering silver Peak countryside, but as I looked back at the town of Hoy it was obscured by a curtain of mist.

Anty Boisjoly Mysteries

Thank you for reading *The Case of the Carnaby Castle Curse*. I hope that even if you managed to figure out who did which murders you had a good time finding out why and how and following an officially record-making number of twists.

The Case of the Carnaby Castle Curse is the fourth Anty Boisjoly mystery and like the preceding (and proceeding) books it's resolutely stand-alone, so if you haven't yet read them all please have a browse below and see if there's something your size.

The Case of the Canterfell Codicil

The first Anty Boisjoly mystery

In The Case of the Canterfell Codicil, Wodehousian gadabout and clubman Anty Boisjoly takes on his first case when his old Oxford chum and coxswain is facing the gallows, accused of the murder of his wealthy uncle. Not one but two locked-room mysteries later, Boisjoly's pitting his wits and witticisms against a subversive butler, a senile footman, a single-minded detective-inspector, an irascible goat, and the eccentric conventions of the pastoral Sussex countryside to untangle a multi-layered mystery of secret bequests, ancient writs, love triangles, revenge, and a teasing twist in the final paragraph.

The Case of the Ghost of Christmas Morning

The Christmas number

In The Case of the Ghost of Christmas Morning, clubman, flaneur, idler and sleuth Anty Boisjoly pits his sardonic wits against another pair of impossible murders. This time, Anty Boisjoly's Aunty Boisjoly is the only possible suspect when a murder victim stands his old friends a farewell drink at the local, hours after being murdered.

The Tale of the Tenpenny Tontine

The dual duel dilemma

It's another mystifying, manor house murder for bon-vivant and problem-solver Anty Boisjoly, when his clubmate asks him to determine who died first after a duel is fought in a locked room. The untold riches of the Tenpenny Tontine are in the balance, but the stakes only get higher when Anty determines that, duel or not, this was a case of murder.

The Case of the Carnaby Castle Curse

The scary one
The ancient curse of Carnaby Castle has begun taking victims again — either that, or someone's very cleverly done away with the new young bride of the philandering family patriarch, and the chief suspect is none other than Carnaby, London's finest club steward.

Anty Boisjoly's wits and witticisms are tested to their frozen limit as he sifts the superstitions, suspicions, and age-old schisms of the mediaeval Peak District village of Hoy to sort out how it was done before the curse can claim Carnaby himself.

Reckoning at the Riviera Royale

The one with Anty's mum
Anty finally has that awkward 'did you murder my father' conversation with his mother while finding himself in the ticklish position of defending her and an innocent elephant against charges of impossible murder.

The Case of the Case of Kilcladdich

The source and origins of Anty's favourite tipple and pastime
Anty Boisjoly travels to the timeless source waters of Glen Glennegie to help decide the fate of his favourite whisky, but an impossible locked room murder is only one of a multitude of mysteries that try Anty's wits and witticisms to their northern limit.

Time trickles down on the traditional tipple as Anty unravels family feuds, ruptured romance, shepherdless sheep, and a series of suspiciously surfacing secrets to sort out who killed whom and how and why and who might be next to die.

The Foreboding Foretelling of Ficklehouse Felling

A manor-house classic stumper reunites Anty
with Wittersham of the Yard

It's a classic, manor house, mystery-within-a-locked-room-mystery for Anty Boisjoly, when a death is foretold by a mystic that Anty's sure is a charlatan. But when an impossible murder follows the foretelling, Anty and his old ally and nemesis Inspector Wittersham must sift the evidence, misguidance, contrivance, and pseudoscience of the household and its haunted history before the killer strikes again.

The Next Anty Boisjoly Mystery

There's almost always a new Anty Boisjoly mystery in the offing, and if you'd like to be kept current to his gadding about, you can sign up for early-bird announcements...

https://indefensiblepublishing.com/books/pj-fitzsimmons/

Made in the USA
Coppell, TX
21 June 2023

18367081R00121